Baby-sitters' Winter Vacation

**Look for these and other books
in the Baby-sitters Club series:**

1 Kristy's Great Idea
2 Claudia and the
      Phantom Phone Calls
3 The Truth About Stacey
4 Mary Anne Saves the Day
5 Dawn and the Impossible Three
6 Kristy's Big Day
7 Claudia and Mean Janine
8 Boy-Crazy Stacey
9 The Ghost at Dawn's House
#10 Logan Likes Mary Anne!
#11 Kristy and the Snobs
#12 Claudia and the New Girl
#13 Good-bye Stacey, Good-bye
#14 Hello, Mallory
#15 Little Miss Stoneybrook
      . . . and Dawn
#16 Jessi's Secret Language
#17 Mary Anne's Bad-Luck Mystery
#18 Stacey's Mistake
#19 Claudia and the Bad Joke
#20 Kristy and the
      Walking Disaster

#21 Mallory and the
      Trouble With Twins
#22 Jessi Ramsey, Pet-sitter
#23 Dawn on the Coast
#24 Kristy and the
      Mother's Day Surprise
#25 Mary Anne and the
      Search for Tigger
#26 Claudia and the
      Sad Good-bye
#27 Jessi and the Superbrat
#28 Welcome Back, Stacey!
#29 Mallory and the
      Mystery Diary

Super Specials:
1 Baby-sitters on Board!
2 Baby-sitters'
      Summer Vacation
3 Baby-sitters'
      Winter Vacation

Baby-sitters' Winter Vacation
Ann M. Martin

AN
APPLE
PAPERBACK

SCHOLASTIC INC.
New York Toronto London Auckland Sydney

Cover art by Hodges Soileau

ISBN 0-590-43973-1

12 11 10 9 8 7 6 5 4   2 3 4 5/9

Printed in the U.S.A.   40

First Scholastic printing, December 1989

For L.G.

Mary Anne's Magical
Winter Adventure
A Book for Logan

Our magical winter
adventure is about to
begin! Tomorrow everyone
in Stoneybrook Middle
School will board buses
and travel to Leicester
Lodge in Hooksett Crossing,
Vermont, for five whole
days. Actually more like

five and a half days.
We leave on Monday
morning and come back
on Saturday afternoon.
The lodge is huge and
beautiful. (I know because
we go there every year.)
It's actually a gigantic
hotel, and it's in the
mountains in an area
with plenty of snow,
which makes it the perfect
place for... Winter Carnival!
I had tons of fun there
last year and the year
before, even though I
didn't want to be part
of the Winter War.

Going to Leicester
Lodge is mandatory. That
means everyone has to go
unless, like you, Logan,
someone has a really,
really good excuse not to.
Even if the trip weren't
mandatory, I'd want
to go. I like having
time for reading and
just being with my

friends. Plus, this year, I volunteered to be the trip historian and do research on Leicester Lodge and Hooksett Crossing. Anyone who volunteers for a special role on the trip gets extra credit in school.

I'm also going to write this book about my adventure and give it to you, since you couldn't come. Your family has had that trip to the darn old island of Aruba planned practically forever. I really wish you could have come to the lodge with us, but since you can't, well, now you can read about our week in Vermont.

So, Logan, this book is for you from me,
Mary Anne.

CHAPTER 1

Mary Anne

Sunday night

I don't believe it. They almost canceled our trip this afternoon! The principal and our teachers, I mean. That's because the weather reports for Vermont have been so bad. Lots of snow is on the way. Even here in Stoneybrook we had a little snow this weekend, which I guess is why the principal panicked.

Anyway, the rumor about the cancellation got started this morning, and by this afternoon, so many parents were

*calling the principal
(at his home) to find
out if it was true
that around 6:00 he
phoned in an announcement
to WSTO saying, "Despite
weather reports, the
Stoneybrook Middle
School trip and Winter
Carnival are still on...."*

Thank goodness we were still going to the lodge. I'd have died if I couldn't have finished my book for Logan. By Sunday, he had already left for Aruba, and if our trip had been canceled, not only would we have had to go to school instead of to the lodge, but the week would have seemed a year long without him. In Vermont I'd be distracted by all the new things to do. In Connecticut, I would just have moped around. Of course, the best thing would have been if Logan could have come to Vermont with us. (He's never even been on the trip because his family still lived in Kentucky last year.) But you can't have everything.

Anyway, by Sunday night the rumor had

been cleared up (or put to rest, as my father would say), so despite the overcast sky and the light snow that was falling, I went to bed knowing the trip was still on.

The trip really is a pretty amazing thing. I don't think kids in many middle schools do what we get to do every year — go away for almost a week at practically no cost. Our parents are just asked to make a donation to the Winter Carnival Fund. If we don't earn enough money, then the Leicester Lodge people cover whatever isn't raised. A nice (rich) couple owns the lodge, and they do this for lots of schools all winter long, just so students can have an away-from-home experience. It's something they like to do for kids. And, boy, do they make our experience nice. Several wings of their huge lodge are equipped as fancy dormitories. (Usually, more than one school is at the lodge at the same time, which is fun because you get to meet new people.) And all week long, they feed us terrific food, and let us use the lodge along with the skiers and other people who are vacationing there. They don't even mind our Winter War.

Before I get too much further along, I better stop and tell you who I am. I'm Mary Anne Spier. I'm thirteen and I'm in eighth grade at

Stoneybrook Middle School (SMS). I don't have any brothers or sisters, just an adorable gray kitten named Tigger. I don't have a mom, either, but I do have a pretty nice dad. We live in Stoneybrook, Connecticut, and I have a lot of friends here. Most of them are my friends in the Baby-sitters Club. Plus, there's Logan (who's also part of the club). He's my boyfriend. It was a long time before I felt brave enough to call him that, but that's what he is.

My friends in the Baby-sitters Club are Kristy Thomas, Dawn Schafer, Claudia Kishi, Stacey McGill, Jessi Ramsey, and Mallory Pike. They were all going on the trip, too. For weeks, the seven of us had been so excited we could hardly say the words "Winter Carnival" without becoming hysterical. Five of us had been on the trip before, but Mal and Jessi hadn't, since they're in sixth grade. It would be their first time.

Kristy and Dawn are my two best friends. Kristy is outgoing and has a big mouth, but I don't mind her mouth — much. She's funny and full of good ideas. She comes from a huge, mixed-up family with brothers, a stepbrother and stepsister, and even an adopted sister. Dawn is an individual. She has somehow learned not to care about what people think, and to just go her own way and do what she wants to do, without hurting anyone's feelings. Dawn has one brother, who lives in California with her father. (Her parents are divorced.)

Claudia and Stacey are best friends, but not *my* best friends, although we're all pretty close. They're both wild dressers, and definitely the most sophisticated of the club members. Stacey even grew up in New York City. One thing you should know about Stacey is that she has diabetes, but she copes really well. Claudia is an artist and a junk-food addict. Stacey's parents are in the middle of a divorce; Claudia's aren't. Stacey is an only child; Claud has an older sister named Janine.

Then there are Jessi and Mal who, by Sunday night, were getting nervous about the trip to the lodge. It wasn't their first time away from home (we all went to Camp Mohawk for two weeks in the summer), but the sixth-graders are always the "babies" of the trip, going away with the "big kids," and that's not an easy position to be in. Anyway, Jessi and Mal are also best friends, and they're big readers, but that's where the similarities end. Mal wants to be a writer when she grows up; Jessi is a talented ballet dancer. Mal has seven younger brothers and sisters; Jessi has two. Also, Mal is white and Jessi is black.

Those are my friends, and I was glad they were all going on the trip with me. (I would have been even happier if Logan were going, though.) At least the trip hadn't been called off. I have to admit that I was kind of surprised by that. When I woke up on Monday the sky was the color of mercury, and the air was heavy with moisture. It was 28° outside, according to our thermometer — perfect snowing weather. And when I tuned into the weather channel on TV, the reports for Vermont were grimmer than ever.

"You better turn on the radio, Mary Anne,"

Dad said to me. "If the trip is off, the cancellation will be announced."

But there was no cancellation, just the report from the night before saying that the trip was still on.

"It's on!" I shouted to Dad.

A good thing, too, since I was dressed, packed, and ready to go.

As soon as Dad and I had finished breakfast, I jumped up from the table and said, "Okay, are you ready to leave?"

"For school?" Dad replied. "Now?"

"Yes."

"It's too early. You'll have to wait for at least half an hour once you reach the school parking lot. And it's not even thirty degrees out."

"I know," I said. "Only twenty-eight. *Please* can't we go? I don't think I can wait a second longer."

"Well, all right," Dad answered. "Brush your teeth and say good-bye to Tigger."

I refrained from reminding him that I'm not a baby. Instead, I just brushed my teeth and then picked up Tigger. All I had to do was look into those shiny eyes of his and I wanted to cry. I could feel a huge lump in my throat.

"Mew?" said Tigger.

"I'll be back on Saturday," I told him. "That's a promise." Then I kissed him on his furry head and set him on the floor. " 'Bye, Tigger."

Tigger went tearing after this plastic ball with a bell in it. He had no idea what was going on.

"Don't forget to feed him," I told Dad about twelve times as we drove through Stoneybrook to SMS. "And change his water. And put that ointment in his eyes if they start to run. And check behind the refrigerator when his toys are missing."

"Yes, ma'am," Dad said good-naturedly.

When he turned the car into the parking lot, I could see that I wasn't the only one who was excited and had wanted to arrive early. About thirty other kids were there, including Kristy, Claudia, and Jessi. I said a nervous good-bye to Dad, hauled my stuff out of the car, and joined my friends. Like me, they were each carrying two duffel bags — except for Claud. Claud was laden down with duffel bags plus all her ski equipment. She is practically a champion skier.

"Doesn't the lodge lend us skis and boots?" I asked. (Not that I was about to go skiing. I am the world's most unathletic person.)

"Yes," Claud replied, "but I wanted to bring my own stuff this year. I ski better with it.

And I plan to help lead the Red Team to victory in the Winter War."

"No way!" cried Kristy. "The Blue Team is going to win!"

The Winter War, I should explain, is the main activity of the Winter Carnival up at the lodge. The week before we left for Vermont, everyone in our school had been randomly assigned to either the Red Team or the Blue Team. The teams would compete in five events during Winter Carnival — an ice-skating contest, a snowball fight, a snow sculpture contest, a downhill skiing competition, and a cross-country skiing competition. Although going to Vermont is mandatory, participating in the war is not. (Thank heavens. I did not plan to participate — even though I wanted my team, the Blue Team, to win.) In case you couldn't tell, Kristy and Claudia were on opposite teams. Kristy was even the *captain* of her team. It was going to be a very competitive week for her.

The four of us were standing, shivering, in the parking lot when Dawn and Mallory arrived, and a few minutes later, Stacey.

"We're all here!" I said. "The Baby-sitters Club is here and ready to go."

"Ready for a week of fun," said Stacey.

"A week of contests," said Kristy.

"A week away from home," said Mal uncertainly.

"A week of relaxation," said Jessi.

"A week of reading and lounging," I said. "I am going to turn into the Leicester Lodge Lounge Lizard."

Everyone laughed. Then Dawn added, "A week of snow."

And Claudia said, "A week of junk-food opportunities. Remember those great candy machines on every floor?"

Dawn, our health-food addict, groaned. "*I* remember the salad bar in the dining hall."

"I'm getting nervous," Mal said suddenly.

"Me, too," agreed Jessi.

"What if we don't *like* the food?" asked Mallory.

"Or spending a week under our teachers' noses?" said Jessi.

"Forget it," answered Claud. "If you survived Camp Mohawk, you can survive any food. Plus, out of school, the teachers don't seem nearly as much like . . . teachers. They just seem like regular adults. After awhile, they sort of blend into the woodwork and you hardly notice them."

"Really?" said Jessi and Mal at the same time.

14

"Really," the rest of us replied.

And at that moment, a huge cheer rose up in the parking lot.

"The buses are here!" someone shouted.

My friends and I turned to look. Good-bye, Connecticut, I thought. Hello, Vermont!

CHAPTER 2

Stacey

Monday

Dear Laine,

Hi. If my writing looks funny, it's because I'm on a bus and the ride is bumpy. We (everyone in school) are on our way to Hooksett Crossing, Vermont, to that lodge I told you about. Can you believe that the population of Hooksett Crossing is only about 2,500? I figured out that there are more than three thousand times that many people in New York City.

Wish me luck in the Winter War. I'm on the Blue Team. Also, keep your fingers crossed that we don't get snowed in up there.

Luv 'n' stuff,
Stacey

The bus ride to Vermont was something else. Luckily, I was prepared for it, having been on the trip in seventh grade. I was also prepared for the good-bye scene with my mother at the school parking lot. It wasn't as bad as I'd thought it would be. There were the usual tears (hers) and the reminders about how to take care of myself, as if I hadn't been doing it for several years already.

"Remember your insulin, honey," she said.

"I will, Mom."

"You did pack your injection kit, didn't you?" (I have to give myself insulin injections every day, in order to control my diabetes. The insulin keeps my blood sugar at a manageable level. If I forget the injections or forget to stick to my diet, my blood sugar goes out of whack, and then I can get really sick.)

"Yup, it's packed," I told Mom. "I never forget it."

"And you'll remind your teacher to remind the cook about your diet?"

"*Yes.*" I was getting impatient. I could see my friends waiting in the parking lot and I was dying to join them.

"Honey, I'm just checking," said Mom. "That's part of my job as a mother."

I smiled. Then I kissed Mom. She let me get

17

out of the car, and I ran to my friends. I knew
that after I met them, when I turned around,
Mom would still be in the parking lot, watching me. So I turned around and waved to her.
She waved back. Then she drove off.

Free at last!

And now we were on the bus. My friends
and I, all seven of us, had managed to get on
the same bus. It was going to be a long trip
to Hooksett Crossing. We weren't due to arrive there until the middle of the afternoon,
weather permitting. But we weren't going to
be on the bus *all* that time. The trip included
two stops, one of which we'd had already.
That was a bathroom break at a rest area on
the highway. Our next stop would be at another rest area, where we could use the bathrooms and eat lunch. I was looking forward
to that break.

But I was getting nervous about the weather.
It had looked like snow for sure in Stoneybrook that morning. And the weather reports
for Vermont included predictions for two
snowstorms, one of which (a small one) was
supposed to hit late in the afternoon. The
teachers were hoping it would hit after we
reached the lodge. The boys were hoping it
would hit before, so we could have some excitement. The girls were divided. Half wanted

18

excitement, the other half wanted to get to the lodge in time for dinner. (The food is pretty good up there, not like at Camp Mohawk.)

I felt someone tap me on the shoulder. It was Kristy, sitting behind me in a seat by herself.

"Stacey?" she said. "I've got a terrible problem."

"What is it?" I asked, alarmed.

"The theme from *Gilligan's Island* is running through my head and I can't get rid of it."

I couldn't help laughing. It didn't matter, since Kristy was laughing, too. Then she said, "I forget, Stace. Are you playing a role in the Winter Carnival?"

I shook my head. "Nope. But I plan to enter every contest in the war. Oh, except cross-country skiing. I've never been on cross-country skis before."

Kristy nodded. Her role in the carnival was going to be a huge one. Not only was she team captain, but she had volunteered to organize the *entire war* — to schedule every practice session and event, to encourage kids to compete (she'd never get Mary Anne), and to help keep score.

"I'm wondering if I made a mistake," said Claud, who was sitting next to me. (We were trying to ignore the bunch of boys in the back

19

of the bus who were singing "I'm Henry the Eighth." Every time they got to the part that went, "Second verse same as the first, a little bit louder and a little bit worse," the *boys* got a little bit louder and a little bit worse. We were waiting for a teacher to notice this and yell at them.)

"A mistake?" I repeated.

Claud nodded. "By agreeing to judge the snow sculpture contest instead of enter it. I really want to make a snow sculpture, but if I did, I couldn't be the judge. It'll be hard enough trying to judge without being partial to the Red Team."

"I think you made the right choice," I told Claud. "The teachers really need you to be the judge." What I didn't say was that Claudia really needed the extra credit she'd earn.

"I guess," said Claud, not sounding at all sure of her decision.

Dawn, Mal, and I were the only club members without extra-credit roles in the Winter Carnival. Mary Anne was going to be the historian, Kristy was going to run the war, Claud was going to judge the snow sculptures, and Jessi was in charge of Talent Night. That meant organizing a whole talent show, helping the kids with their acts, arranging for rehearsals, and more. This year was the first time the role had been given to a sixth-grader, but we all knew Jessi could handle it.

Then there were Dawn and Mal and I. Dawn and I simply hadn't found any roles that interested us. Mal, on the other hand, had brought along a project of her own — her journal. I wasn't sure exactly what she planned to do with it, but she'd said it was going to keep her busy.

"Hey, Mary Anne," I said suddenly, leaning across the aisle.

"Yeah?" Mary Anne was busy ducking. The boys in the back were throwing wadded-up gum wrappers all over the bus. The teachers, however, had noticed — finally — and had decided that the boys' restlessness meant that it was time to stop for lunch. Luckily, the chosen rest area was just a few miles away.

"How are you going to research the history of the lodge and the town?" I asked Mary Anne.

"Oh, the teachers said there's plenty of information right in the lodge's library. Plus, a lot of people who work at the lodge grew up in Hooksett Crossing, and some of them are pretty old. They'll have information, too."

"That doesn't sound so bad," I said.

Mary Anne shook her head — and ducked

again. And just then, the bus started to slow down. It rounded a corner and ahead of us, off to the right, I could see a large rest area. Several school buses (ours!) had already pulled into the parking lot. We followed them and parked in a row. Then the buses began to empty out, and us SMS students (all 382 of us) trooped inside this building and into what must have been the world's largest cafeteria. Honestly, it looked just like our school cafeteria, only bigger. It was not the same place where we'd eaten lunch on last year's trip to the lodge.

"What I can't figure out," I said to Claud as we stepped inside, "is why the people behind the counters look so horrified. You'd think they'd be glad to have our business. Besides, don't you suppose they're used to large groups of people? Their parking lot is the size of Texas. So is their restaurant."

"Maybe they're not used to *this* big a group," replied Claud.

Anyway, what the frantic restaurant workers didn't know was that most of us had brought our own lunches and just needed places to sit down. We found them quickly. The room was full of tables, and soon the tables were full of us.

My friends and I grabbed a big round table

for ourselves. We dumped out our lunches, began to eat — and for the next half hour were up and down in our seats like jack-in-the-boxes. First Kristy got napkins for us, then Mal decided she wanted a soda, then I decided the same thing, then Jessi bought an orange, then Claud spotted a tray of Twinkies, and so forth. It was the most un-peaceful meal imaginable. I was glad to get back on the bus, even knowing that the boys had plans to start singing "John Jacob Jingleheimer Schmidt."

As the kids in our school trooped out of the restaurant, every single worker let out a huge

23

sigh of relief. It was as if the building went, "Whoosh," as we walked outside into the . . . snow!

Snow had started to fall while we were eating.

Several kids let out yells. Someone shouted, "Hooray! We're going to be snowbound at Leicester Lodge!"

"Really?" asked Jessi nervously as us BSC members boarded our bus.

"I doubt it," I replied, but I wasn't sure.

It had only been snowing for ten or fifteen minutes and already the ground was white. Although the time was 1:15 in the afternoon, the sky had begun to grow dark. We ran for our seats, everyone scrambling to sit next to the windows in order to watch the storm as closely as possible.

"Are we going to turn back?" Alan Gray shouted to the teachers. (The teachers were up near the front of the bus in a huddle.)

"No," one teacher replied. "We're much closer to Hooksett Crossing than to Stoney-brook."

So we drove slowly toward Leicester Lodge.

By three o'clock we were way behind schedule. The roads were treacherous. The wind and the snow were blowing hard and the drivers of the buses (we tried to stick together —

a convoy of SMS students) had to crawl along
at a snail's pace. The bus was quiet as everyone strained to watch the road.

We were just ten miles from Hooksett Crossing when a deer leaped in front of our bus.

Immediately our driver slammed on the
brakes. We missed the deer but we rammed
into a snowy embankment on the side of the
road.

Everyone screamed. Claudia and I clasped
hands.

By some miracle no one was hurt, and also
the bus in back of us stayed where it be-
longed — on the road. The driver of that bus
pulled ahead of us, parked, then got out to
give our driver a hand backing up. Ten minutes later we were on the road again.

When someone on the silent bus finally said
in a hushed voice, "Ooh, *there's* the lodge," I
nearly cried, I was so relieved.

Claud looked at me. "We're here," she said.

"Yeah," I replied. "Lodge sweet lodge."

CHAPTER 3

Dawn

Monday

Dear Dad and Jeff,

Boy, did we have some adventure getting to Leicester Lodge today. On the way to Vermont a snowstorm hit and the driving got really bad. Then a deer jumped in front of the bus and our driver ran into a snowbank. No one was hurt, but were we ever scared. A bunch of kids started to cry, including some boys. (Also Mary Anne, who was sitting next to me.) Don't worry. We got to the lodge (which is huge) safe *and sound, just late and nervous. Now the fun can begin!*

Love and Sunshine,
Dawn

W hen we finally reached the lodge, darkness had fallen, and the lodge was all lit up. It was snow-covered, too, and looked just like a scene on a Christmas card — the flakes still falling, the silvery-dark sky, and the yellow glow of the lodge.

The people who run the lodge, Mr. and Mrs. George, were really nice to us. We had arrived late and they knew we'd been delayed by the storm. Then they heard about the accident. They were terribly sympathetic. Mrs. George clucked over all of us — teachers, too — like a mother hen as we stepped inside the lodge. Then she began directing us SMS students to various dorms.

Mal gasped. "Ohhh," I heard her say softly as she got her first look at the inside of Leicester Lodge.

I know why she drew her breath in like that. It's because, although the lodge looks big from the outside, you don't *feel* its vastness until you're inside. Have you ever seen that Stephen King movie *The Shining*? Remember the Overlook Hotel, where all the scary things happened? Remember how big it was? Well, that's pretty much the way the lodge looks. I mean, it's just wing after wing, floor after floor, room after room. Most of the left end of the lodge is made up of dormitories (as opposed to rooms or suites), and that's where Mrs. George took us.

"Three other groups of kids will be here this week," she told us. "One is the eighth-graders from a junior high in northern Vermont, another is the seventh- and eighth-graders from a middle school in New Hampshire, and we're still expecting a group of elementary school children from Maine."

Goody, I thought. I like meeting new people.

After walking for what seemed like miles, Mrs. George and the teachers began directing large groups of us into various dorms. Each room was so big it could sleep fifty-six people — two rows of fourteen bunk beds each.

"Bunk beds," moaned Stacey. "I'd forgotten. Just like at Camp Mohawk."

"No, *not* just like at Camp Mohawk," I replied. "At camp we didn't have dressers or a rug on the floor or mirrors on the wall."

"Or adjoining bathrooms," added Kristy.

"How am I ever going to find my way around?" wailed Mal as the BSC members, still in a group, continued to follow Mrs. George down the hall.

"We'll have to leave a trail of bread crumbs," said Jessi.

I glanced at Mary Anne and grinned. Then I said, "No, you won't. Really. Last year was my first year here and I thought the same th — "

"Okay, the remaining sixth-grade girls, into this room," called Mr. Bailey, an English teacher.

"They're grouping us by *grades!*" exclaimed Mal in dismay.

We'd been so busy talking we hadn't noticed.

"Did they break us up by grade last year?" I asked Mary Anne.

"I don't remember. I guess so. Anyway, it didn't matter because the BSC members were all in the same grade," she replied.

We said a sad good-bye to Jessi and Mal (I really thought Mal was going to cry), then the last hundred or so of us continued down the hall. We stopped to separate the seventh-grade boys from the eighth-grade girls when we reached the boys' dorm, and then us girls were shown into a final room. Our school filled seven dorms altogether.

Mary Anne, Stacey, Claud, Kristy, and I entered our room.

"Hello, room," said Kristy, who was getting punchy.

"Our home for the next five days," I added.

It really was a very nice room, except for the bunks. But even the bunk beds were a lot nicer than the ones at camp, which looked like someone had tossed a bunch of trees into the cabins and carved the beds out of them right there.

A soft tan carpet covered the floor, and next to each set of bunks was a dresser. Over the dresser was a mirror, and —

"There're the bathrooms!" announced Kristy, pointing to a door at one end of the room.

A few girls dropped their bags and made a dash for the bathrooms. The rest of us scrambled to claim bunk beds. Mary Anne and I got one. (My mom is going out with Mary Anne's dad, and we figured that being bunkies would be good practice in case we ever wound up as stepsisters.) Next to us were Stacey and Claud. Poor Kristy was left without a bunkie and looked sort of sorry for herself.

Then she began to wonder if she would even

need a bunkie. "Maybe there are only fifty-four or fifty-five of us," she said excitedly. "I could have a whole bunk to myself. I could sleep on the top tonight, the bottom tomorrow night, the top the third night, the — "

"I don't have a bunkie, Kristy," said a voice from behind us.

Kristy turned around. There was Ashley Wyeth, this spacey, artsy friend of Claudia's. She doesn't have too many good friends besides Claud.

"You don't?" said Kristy. She wanted to be polite, but she couldn't help looking crestfallen.

None of us was sure what to do until Claudia said tactfully, "Hey, why don't Stacey and I move down one bunk, and then Kristy, you and Ashley can be right between Dawn and Mary Anne, and Stacey and me."

"Okay." Kristy managed not to sound *too* reluctant. Then, brightening, she added, "Hey, Ashley, can I have the top bunk?"

Ashley shrugged. "Sure."

Kristy didn't have to worry. Ashley would be a pushover to bunk with. Besides, how could Kristy lose, surrounded by all her friends?

"Come on, you guys, let's unpack," said Stacey. "Then we can go exploring. We don't have to be anywhere until six-thirty, when they serve dinner."

"Go exploring?" I repeated. "We already know where everything is."

"Yeah, but Mal and Jessi don't. And they looked sort of, oh, terrified when we left them. I thought we could give them a tour."

I smiled at Stacey. "Good idea."

So the five of us unpacked quickly. Then we got ready to find the sixth-grade girls' dorm. Claud asked Ashley if she wanted to come with us, but Ashley was sprawled on the floor, sketching. She barely heard the question. We found our way to Mal and Jessi's room and were greeted by cries of, "You found us!" and, "We knew you'd come back!"

I couldn't help laughing. "You guys are supposed to be having *fun*," I pointed out.

"How can we have fun when we don't even know where we are?" asked Mal.

"Look, I'll give you a hint," said Mary Anne. "Every floor is the same, except for the main floor, so you can quit worrying about floors two through four. They're all rooms or dorms. Just learn the way from your dorm to the first floor, okay?"

"Let's go all the way upstairs," said Claud as the seven of us walked into the hallway. "Then we'll work our way down and prove to them that the second, third, and fourth floors are all the same."

We decided that was a good idea, and took the elevator to the fourth floor.

"See?" I said when the doors opened. "This is just like our floor, the second floor."

"By the way, there's the fourth-floor, D-wing candy machine," added Claud.

We rode to the third floor. "There's the third-floor, D-wing candy machine," said Claud.

We rode to the second floor. "There's *our* candy machine," said Claud.

We rode to the first floor. "There's the dining hall," said Claud as we got off the elevator.

"Home of Claudia's favorite salad bar," I added.

Claud scrunched up her nose and made a horrible face.

"Anyway," said Kristy to Jessi and Mal, "now you know how to get from your dorm to the dining hall."

"Do we have to ride up and look at all the candy machines each time?" asked Jessi, and the rest of us laughed.

"Now we'll show you the really fun stuff," I said. "Follow this hallway in this direction and you come to . . . the common room. This is the main room of the lodge. The check-in desk is here, but it's also a gathering area."

"Look at the fireplace!" said Jessi. "It's so big."

"This is a beautiful room," added Mal.

She was right. The common room was a long, lofty room with beams in the ceiling. It was built of brick and wood. Tables and chairs were grouped for playing board games or cards. There were big easy chairs for reading in. Under our feet was a woolly carpet. Kids and teachers were already drifting down from the dorms. Some of the other guests were finding seats near the fire.

It was just when Jessi was suggesting that we continue the tour that the front door to the lodge burst open, blowing snow onto the carpet, and two nearly frozen people, a man and a woman, staggered inside. The man immediately collapsed on the ground.

"Oh, my lord!" cried Claudia.

A whole bunch of hotel workers rushed to help the people. Someone slammed the door shut. Everyone was asking questions. Finally the woman said, "You've got to help us. Please. We had an accident about two miles down the road. Our bus overturned. We — "

"Bus?" said Mrs. George, making her way through the crowd. "You're not from Conway Cove Elementary School, are you?"

"Yes! We are!" said the woman. "You must be Mrs. George." (Mrs. George nodded.) "Anyway, I think all the children are okay," the woman went on, "but my arm is fractured — at least, I'm pretty sure it is — and Jim — "

"Jim is going to be fine," spoke up the man on the floor. "I just needed to warm up." He raised his head a little. Then, tentatively, he pulled himself into a sitting position. "See? I'm okay. But we have to get some help back to the kids. They're alone with the bus driver, and he's not in very good shape. He'll need an ambulance. His leg is broken — badly."

"How did you get here?" asked Mrs. George.

"We walked," said the man.

"For two miles? In this weather?" Mrs. George was amazed. And everyone looked outside at the storm, which was growing worse by the second. Then Mrs. George said, "We'll call the police and the rescue squad right away."

Mary Anne and I looked at each other, stunned.

CHAPTER 4

Kristy

Monday evening

Dear Mom, Watson, Nannie, Sam, Charlie, David Michael, Emily, Andrew, and Karen:

Boy, did the Winter Carnival ever get off to an exciting start. There were two bus accidents today. Tomorrow we hold practices for the Winter War events, and the war begins on Wednesday. This is our schedule:

Wed.

ice-skating-a.m.
snow sculpture-p.m.

Thurs.

snowball fight

Fri.

downhill skiing-a.m.
x-country skiing-p.m.

Love You Lots, Kristy

Talk about excitement. I was beginning to think that maybe we were having too much of it. When that teacher fell through the doorway to the lodge, I thought I'd faint. And then the other teacher started talking about the children and the accident.

I have to say that the Georges remained calm and took charge of things very well. While Mr. George phoned the police and the rescue squad, Mrs. George helped the teachers onto a sofa and phoned the hotel doctor.

"We have to drive back to the accident," the woman teacher was saying.

"Oh, no," said Mrs. George. "Not you. Not either of you. But I'll have my husband start our bus and he and I and a couple of other teachers — we've got plenty here — " she added with a smile, "can go back to the accident and meet the ambulance. Then we'll bring the kids here."

While Mrs. George was talking, my brain was clicking along. I was getting an idea.

"Do we have any volunteers to brave the storm?" Mrs. George asked the crowd that had gathered. "Teachers would be best, I think."

Before anyone could answer, I stepped forward and opened my big mouth. "We'll go," I said. "The Baby-sitters Club will go."

"The . . . what?" Mrs. George looked flustered for the first time.

"The Baby-sitters Club. Us," I said simply, gesturing to my friends.

My math teacher stepped forward. "They're great with kids," he said. "They'd probably be a good choice." (We have a wide reputation.)

Mrs. George looked at the seven of us. "Well . . . terrific," she said finally. "I think some adults should go along, too, though."

In the end, the Georges, three SMS teachers,

and my friends and I were the ones who helped rescue the children. We scrambled into our warmest clothes and then piled onto the old school bus that was waiting in front of the lodge. Mr. George was behind the steering wheel.

"We bought this bus eight years ago," Mrs. George told us. "Our son thought we were crazy, but it's come in handy more than once."

The bus pulled onto the road and drove slowly in the direction of the accident. Mrs. George gave us some instructions. Then everyone on board grew silent. I tried to read the expressions on the faces of my friends, but it was too dark to see. I knew the club members were nervous but in control. Not one of them minded that I had volunteered our services. Children come first where we're concerned, and we've handled pretty many emergencies, as well as large groups of children. This was something we *had* to do.

The bus drove slowly along. Mr. George wouldn't go faster than fifteen miles an hour because he didn't want us to crash, too. At long last I saw flashing red lights ahead.

"Look!" I said softly, nudging Dawn.

"Oh, wow." Dawn strained forward to see what was going on.

Mr. George drew the bus to a slow halt. Then he said, "Okay, everyone out. Help in any manner you think is necessary, but don't get in the way of the rescue workers."

We piled out of the bus and surveyed the scene. The police and rescue squad were already there. An ambulance, a tow truck, and three squad cars were parked by the side of the road. Flares had been set up around the bus, so we had a pretty good look at the accident itself. The bus seemed to have skidded off the road and down a short embankment before rolling over on its side.

We arrived just as the paramedics were struggling up the embankment, carrying a stretcher with the bus driver on it. Huddled around the bus were the children. There were sixteen of them. And every single one of them was crying. A police officer was trying to calm them, but she wasn't having much luck.

"Okay, you guys," I said to the other members of the BSC. "There are sixteen kids and seven of us. Let's each take two or three and try to quiet them down, okay?"

"Okay," said Dawn, Jessi, Mal, Mary Anne, Stacey, and Claud in one voice.

We trudged down the embankment, holding hands when we needed to. The ground was incredibly slippery and the wind was howling and blowing snow in our faces so that it was difficult to see.

When we reached the kids, we didn't waste a second. I took the first two I saw and separated them from the others. (The police officer looked relieved.)

I had grabbed a boy and a girl. The boy was about eight and the girl was maybe seven. Neither one was wearing a hat, and the boy was missing a glove.

"Hi," I said to them. I squatted down in the snow so I was closer to their height. "My name is Kristy. Guess what. I'm staying at the lodge. The same place where you're going. Boy, did you have a scary accident."

"It was awful," wailed the girl.

"The bus driver is *dead*," added the boy.

"No, he isn't," I assured them. "He looked pretty bad, but your teacher said he just broke his leg. Honest. Now listen, it's freezing out here. Where are your hats? And where's your other glove?" I asked the boy. I took his bare hand in my mittens and rubbed it briskly.

"They came off when the bus fell over," said the boy. "Pinky even lost her shoe."

"Pinky? Who's Pinky?" I said. The children already seemed calmer and I was glad.

"Pinky's that girl over there," answered the boy, pointing.

I looked around and saw that Stacey was carrying one of her kids in order to keep her shoeless foot out of the snow. She was trying to warm the foot by wrapping it in someone's knitted hat.

"Oh," I said. "Listen, what are your names? I told you mine, but I don't know yours."

"I'm Bryce," said the boy.

"I'm Ginnie," said the girl.

"Okay. Bryce and Ginnie. Bryce, you keep your bare hand in your pocket, okay?"

Bryce nodded.

"Now listen," I went on. "Is either one of you hurt? Do you hurt anywhere?"

The kids shook their heads.

"Are you sure?"

"Yup," said Ginnie. Then she asked in a wavery voice, her eyes starting to fill with tears again, "What's going to happen now?"

Mrs. George had explained that to us on the way to the scene of the accident. With the nearest hospital almost thirty miles away, we were just going to take the kids back to the lodge and let the doctor there check them over, unless any of them looked seriously injured or had been knocked unconscious or something. Luckily, all the kids seemed to be fine, just cold and scared.

"We're going to drive back to the lodge and get you guys warmed up," I said. "There's a big fire going in the fireplace, and it's almost suppertime. Oh, and I know a secret about the cook at Leicester Lodge."

"What?" said Bryce and Ginnie eagerly.

"He makes the *best* hot chocolate in the *world*," I whispered.

"Really?" asked Ginnie, intrigued.

"Really."

By this time most of the kids had stopped crying, and the teachers had gathered up all the loose things — hats and shoes and gloves and lunch boxes — from the crash site that they could find. Now a police officer had managed to climb inside the crippled bus and was handing suitcases through the windows to the Georges.

Very quickly, the teachers, the children, their gear, and us BSC members were back on the Georges' bus, the heater going full blast.

Before we left, Mrs. George pulled something out of her pocket. It turned out to be a list of all the children who were supposed to be on the bus. The teacher with the fractured arm had given it to her. Mrs. George took a roll call and two head counts before she'd let her husband start up the bus.

Pretty smart, I thought.

The teachers were sitting in the back of the bus with the kids' suitcases and armloads of loose things they'd found in the snow. It's amazing how much stuff sixteen little kids can get on a bus for a simple five-day vacation.

My friends and I and the children were sitting closer to the front. We were crowded three or four across in the seats. We could have spread out more, but the kids were so frightened that they'd become clingy and wouldn't let us BSC members out of their sight. Some of them wouldn't even let go of our hands.

As we plowed slowly through the snow back to the lodge, Mary Anne spoke up. "You guys?"

"Yes?" said the rest of us club members.

"Could you do me a favor? You know the book I'm making for Logan?"

"Yes?" we said again.

"Well, considering what's just happened, I have a feeling this is going to be an . . . unusual week. I want Logan to know what *really* goes on. I mean, not just from my point of view. So do you think you could each make a few notes every day? Just jot down things that happen — to you or to anyone else. Whatever you think is important."

"Sure," the rest of us replied.

"Oh, great," said Mary Anne. "Then I'll collect your notes at the end of each day and try to blend everything together so that Logan has a — " Mary Anne stopped talking. She pointed to me and I looked down at my sides.

Bryce and Ginnie were sound asleep. They were leaning heavily against me. The other children were falling asleep, too. My friends and I stopped talking. We rode to the lodge in silence.

CHAPTER 5

Claudia

monday nigt

Hi, Mary anne these are my notes four you.

Well I have never seen little childern wake up so fast. One minut they were sleeping on the bus the next minut they were in the loge and wide awake. First the loge docter checked the kids. Then we ate dinner. We were all straving. After that we had to ~~figy~~ figure (stacey helped me spell that) out waht to do whith the kids since there teachers were at the hospitle....

Everything happened awfully quickly after
we reached the lodge again (safely, I might
add). As we pulled up to the front door, Kristy
said softly, "Wake up, you guys. We're here."

Well, those kids looked up sleepily — and
then they came to life! They tore off the bus
and through the front door, which Mrs.
George held open for them. Then Pinky, the
little girl who was wearing a hat on her foot,
came to a screeching halt and began yelling,
"Miss Weber! Mr. Dougherty! Where are
you?"

Of course, a crowd gathered. Everyone
wanted to see "the poor little children who'd
been in the horrible bus accident." (I actually
heard one woman say that.) Luckily Mr.
George appeared around the same time that
my friends and I caught up to the kids.

Mr. George told them straightforwardly that
Miss Weber and Mr. Dougherty, the two
teachers who had braved the snow, had been
taken to the hospital to get patched up, but
that they'd only be there overnight.

"What about us?" wailed Joey, one of the
kids I was watching.

Good question. I looked at the Georges.
They were looking at each other. Finally Mrs.
George said, "First the doctor wants to check

you over. Then I think we should eat dinner. It was served over an hour ago. I'm hungry. How about you?"

We were starved, which is not good for Stacey. With her diabetes, she shouldn't skip meals. It messes up her blood sugar or something. The kids were hungry, too, after their adventure. So after the doctor had given them a clean bill of health, everyone from the bus went into the dining hall. We sat at two of the long tables. The BSC members scattered themselves among the children, in order to give them a hand if they needed it. When the food came we *gobbled* it down. That's how hungry we were. And since, unlike the cooks at camp, the head cook here is nice and really listens to people, there was no food served (except dessert) that Stacey couldn't eat. (The Camp Mohawk cook kept serving sugary stuff, like candied yams, that Stacey's not allowed to eat.)

Anyway, when dinner was over, Mrs. George turned the sixteen kids over to the cook, who took them into the kitchen to show them how he and his helpers prepare food for hundreds of people every day. As soon as they were gone, Mrs. George said to the rest of us, who were still sitting at the dining tables, "I want to thank you so much for your help tonight. You don't *know* how my husband and I appreciate it. Lots of groups of students visit the lodge each winter, but nothing like this has ever happened."

"I hate to bring this up," said Mr. Cheney, one of the SMS teachers, "but what about the kids? What are they going to do now?"

Mrs. George sat down. "I'm not sure," she said. "They'll stay here tonight, of course. We can't send them back to Maine in this weather, particularly not without their teachers. But I guess they could go back tomorrow. I hate to deprive them of this trip, though. They won it."

"They won it?" I repeated.

Mrs. George nodded. "Their school sponsored a readathon. These are the winners. They worked hard and they've really been looking forward to this. They come from a small town and most of their families don't have much money. This is the first time some of them have been away from Conway Cove. We'll have to call their parents tonight to tell them what happened. I'm sure the children will want to talk to them anyway. Maybe after a few phone calls we'll have a better idea of what to do with the kids. The school might be able to send down some parents to act as chaperones or something. Thank goodness none of the kids is hurt. They could easily stay here if we can just find someone to keep an eye on them."

"What about the teachers who went to the hospital?" said Mr. Cheney. "Won't they be back tomorrow?"

Mr. George answered that question. "Yes, but they'll be out of commission, at least for any activities such as skiing or skating. As you know, Miss Weber broke her arm. And the doctor here at the lodge thought Mr. Dougherty might have cracked several ribs."

At this point I nudged Kristy.

"Huh?" she said. She'd been deep in thought.

"We could help," I whispered. "We could watch the kids."

Kristy smiled. "Exactly what I was thinking. Should I say something?"

"Nothing ever stopped you before."

Ooh. If looks could kill . . . But Kristy tried to forget what I'd said. She stood up slowly.

"Excuse me," she said. "I have an idea." She glanced from Stacey to Jessi to Mal to Dawn to Mary Anne, silently asking their permission to volunteer our services. My friends nodded. "Well," Kristy went on, "my friends and I could take care of the kids this week."

"We could even bunk with them," I added.

51

"We could just move our stuff into another dorm and bunk with the kids."

"Well, that would be wonderful," replied Mrs. George, "but I don't know. It's up to your teachers."

"I don't know, either," said Mr. Cheney, and I felt myself deflate like a balloon with a hole in it. "Do you girls really want to give up your vacation?" he asked.

"I don't think we'd be giving it up," said Kristy. "If Miss Weber and Mr. Dougherty can help watch the kids while they're indoors, we can just include the children in our regular activities. We'll take turns doing special things with them. We won't mind. The kids can even come to our talent show."

"Or be *in* it!" said Jessi excitedly.

"We're used to kids, believe me," added Kristy.

"You're sure this is something you *want* to do?" asked Mr. Cheney. "It's not playtime, you know. It's a big responsibility — and it's for five days."

"We know and we're sure," said Kristy firmly.

"Right," agreed the rest of us club members.

"The lodge would be glad to pay you for your help," spoke up Mrs. George.

That time, Kristy didn't even need to look at the rest of us for our opinions. "Thanks," she replied, "but that's okay. We don't need to be paid. We're still going to have a great time here. Besides, every year, you and Mr. George let our whole school come visit and I know we never pay you enough for it. The least we can do is help out some of the other kids you're giving a treat to."

Well, Kristy should know better than to say something like that to an adult. Of course Mrs. George began to cry because she was so touched. Us BSC members decided it was time to hightail it out of there. Besides, the cook was bringing the children back.

When Mrs. George recovered, she showed us to an empty dorm room. While my friends and I gathered our possessions and moved them into the kids' room, Mrs. George and the children called their parents, and the SMS teachers carried the children's belongings to the room. As soon as they left, we decided to get the kids ready for bed. First, though, we had to sort out that mountain of loose caps and mittens and things. We spent nearly half an hour holding up one item at a time, saying, "Whose is this?" and waiting for someone to call out, "Mine!"

When everything was finally organized, Kristy said, "Okay, you guys, change into your pajamas."

I have never heard such screaming in my life. Uh-oh — we were in a coed dorm! The boys wouldn't change in front of the girls and the girls wouldn't change in front of the boys. And neither group trusted the other to close their eyes or turn their backs. Finally we worked out an arrangement. Since there were fewer boys, they could change in the bathroom while us girls changed in the dorm. The boys were on their honor not to come out of the bathroom until we said it was okay. Even so, the girls changed clothes as if they were on their way to a fire.

At long last, each of our charges was tucked in bed.

Ahhh, I thought as my friends and I climbed wearily into *our* beds. No sooner were the covers pulled up and the lights turned off than a little voice said, "Stacey? My foot hurts. It didn't hurt before, but now it does."

It was Pinky. Stacey got out of bed and looked at Pinky's foot. She thought it seemed swollen so she called the lodge doctor, who arrived pronto, examined Pinky's foot, pronounced her ankle slightly sprained (undoubtedly as a result of the crash), bandaged it, and told her to stay off of it the next day. Then he quickly looked over the other kids again and found them fine but sleepy.

When he left, I turned off the lights for a second time. "Good night, everybody," I said.

" 'Night, Claudia," said a chorus of voices. Then all the children began saying good night to each other, one at a time. That was an awful lot of "good nights," but my friends and I let them go to it because we knew they were still nervous and frightened.

It was eleven o'clock before the last of us fell asleep.

CHAPTER 6

Mary Anne

Tuesday

When we woke up the next morning, the snow was still falling. It was funny, Logan. I should have been excited about the day that lay ahead, but I couldn't work up any enthusiasm. All I could think about was you and Aruba and whatever you were doing down there. I guess there are a lot of beautiful girls on an island like that.

To take my mind off of those thoughts, I concentrated on the sixteen children my friends and I were caring for. Their parents had given them permission to *stay at the lodge as planned, so now they really were our charges. (Teachers don't bunk with students. They have their own suites.)*

I wondered what the day would bring.

I awoke very slowly and groggily the next morning. It's amazing how much a few out-of-the-ordinary events can drain you. I realized I was still tired, even though we'd gotten plenty of sleep the night before.

I peered around our semidark room. Mrs. George had put us in a small, oddly shaped dorm. There were just twelve bunks in it. Dawn and I were bunkies again, so were Jessi and Mal, and so were Stacey and Claud. Kristy had thought she had another chance for a bunk all to herself since there was an uneven number of us, but no such luck. Apparently, none of the kids wanted to bunk with Pinky, so Pinky ended up bunking alone, and Kristy shared with Ginnie, who seemed pretty attached to her.

Around me the kids were still sound asleep. I glanced at Claudia, Kristy, and Stacey. They

57

were dead to the world. I leaned over my bed and peered down at Dawn. She was snoring.

It should have been a happy morning. Outside, the snow was still falling — heavily. I *love* snow, but for some reason I couldn't work up any enthusiasm over it. I knew that downstairs the cooks were preparing a big, yummy breakfast, and I was hungry, but I couldn't work up any enthusiasm over breakfast, either. Furthermore, I was pretty sure the kids would wake up in good spirits, since they'd been fairly perky by bedtime the night before, and *very* excited about the prospect of skiing and skating that day.

But I just didn't feel . . . I don't know. Something was nagging at me. I couldn't put my finger on it.

I looked at my watch. It read seven-thirty. Breakfast would be served at eight. I climbed out of bed, wishing that I'd gotten the bottom bunk instead of the top, but Dawn had claimed the bottom right away — in both our old dorm and the one we'd moved into the night before.

I turned on the lights in the room.

All around me I heard moaning and groaning.

"How can it be morning already?" mumbled Claud.

"I could sleep forever," added Jessi.

"Me, too," echoed Mal. "Forever and *ever*."

"It's still snowing," I announced, trying to sound cheerful. "Look outside. It's a fairyland. All you can see is white."

Kristy was the only one who looked outside. *"Oh,"* she said, sounding incredibly depressed. "If this keeps up, we won't be able to hold practices today. What a drag. The events start tomorrow. We *have* to practice."

"Cool your jets," said Dawn. "People are always skiing when it's snowing. And I'm sure someone from the lodge will clear off the skating pond."

"I guess," Kristy replied distractedly.

"Well, come *on*, everybody," I said loudly. "Up and at 'em. Twenty minutes until breakfast."

Our sleepy charges aroused themselves slowly. The boys looked like zombies as they headed for the bathroom. But the girls came to life quickly and dressed in record time, afraid that the boys would come out of the bathroom before we'd given them the all-clear signal.

The kids were dressed and in the process of making up their beds when a knock sounded at our door.

"Come in!" called Kristy.

And into our room stepped . . . dum da-dum dum . . . Ms. Halliday — my most feared teacher at SMS. She teaches seventh-grade girls' gym, and last year she'd been the bane of my existence. I couldn't stand her and she couldn't stand me. That's because Ms. Halliday doesn't like klutzes. And I am a total klutz. I am absolutely no good at sports, which is why I was not taking part in the Winter War.

As you can probably imagine, though, Kristy and Ms. Halliday get along extremely well. Usually, gym instructors don't have teachers' pets, but Ms. Halliday was an exception. Her pet had been Kristy, the great athlete of the world, and they were still friends this year, even though Ms. Halliday was no longer Kristy's teacher.

Anyway, when she poked her head into our room, I just froze. It was like the beginning of another dreaded volleyball game. I could almost hear her saying, "Okay, Mary Anne, *serve.* . . . No, *over* the net, *over* the net. Use a little power. Put some muscle into it."

But of course that was not what Ms. Halliday said. Instead, she said, "In all the confusion last night, I forgot to tell you kids that I'm one of your dorm supervisors. The others will be Miss Weber and Mr. Dougherty, as soon as they return from the hospital. The three of us will help you with the Conway

Cove students. That's what we're here for, okay? I can give them a hand with outdoor activities and the others can oversee indoor activities. That way, you members of the Baby-sitters Club will be able to have some time to yourselves."

"Thanks, Ms. Halliday!" exclaimed Kristy.

Ms. Halliday left then and my friends and I helped the little kids with last-minute chores — shoe-tying, hair-braiding, etc. I did everything mechanically, like a robot who has been programmed to perform. When we were ready, we left our dorm and Kristy showed the kids the way downstairs to the dining hall. (Claudia showed them the candy machine.)

The twenty-three of us filed into breakfast and chose a table to ourselves. We ate hungrily — scrambled eggs, toast, and fruit. And after that, we were on our own. The snow was letting up, and Kristy had announced skiing practice for the morning. The Conway Cove kids were eager to try skiing, so Ms. Halliday bundled them up (except for Pinky) and took them off to one of the beginners' lessons.

By ten o'clock in the morning, I found myself pretty much on my own. Kristy, Claud, Dawn, and Stacey had hit the slopes, Mallory was off doing something with her secret journal project, and Jessi had volunteered to entertain Pinky for the day, since Pinky was under doctor's orders to stay inside with her foot up. If the pain and swelling in her ankle were gone by the evening, then she would be able to do whatever she wanted the next day.

What should I do with myself? I wondered. Even though I didn't really feel like working, I decided I might as well get on with my job as historian for the Winter Carnival. There were only four days in which to do my research. Once I returned to Stoneybrook, I had to be ready to write up the project. I certainly wasn't going to be able to do any research on tiny Hooksett Crossing or on Leicester Lodge anywhere but here.

So I went upstairs to our dorm, found a pad of paper and a pen, and went back downstairs to the room next to the common room. It was the Leicester Lodge library.

The books in the library are just there for the guests to read and enjoy. Most of them are novels, mysteries, and skiing guides, but on a shelf near a ceiling-to-floor window, I found two rows of books on local history. I looked at a few of the titles: *A Brief History of Hookset Crossing*, *Rutledge County: A Retrospective*, *Ski Resorts in Vermont*. There were quite a few more, too. Most of them were written by local authors and published by small Vermont presses. Then one title caught my eye: *Leicester Lodge: 1920 to 1980*, by Thomas George. Thomas George . . . could that be Mr. George? I checked the book jacket. It was! His picture was there and everything.

Well. The teachers had been right. There was plenty of information for my report. I pulled several books off the shelf, piled them on an end table, and curled up in an armchair to start taking a few notes. Most of the books covered boring things like population statistics, agricultural information, weather and weather patterns, plus a lot of stuff about how to make maple syrup. But nearly every book mentioned one chilling story: the tale of the ghost of Leicester Lodge.

My heart began to pound. I hadn't heard about any ghost before. Why hadn't last year's historian uncovered this information? Then I remembered. There hadn't been a historian the year before. No one had volunteered for the job. No one had volunteered when I was in sixth grade, either. It took a dork like me to volunteer. No wonder the teachers had been so thrilled when I'd raised my hand.

I shivered. The ghost of Leicester Lodge. Did Mr. George mention it in his book? He certainly did. He devoted three entire chapters to it, finally concluding that there was no ghost — there were just a lot of people with big imaginations.

Immediately, I ran to the kitchen to interview the cook and some of the hotel workers.

"Is there a ghost at the lodge?" I asked the cook breathlessly.

"Some say so," he replied cryptically.

"Well, have you ever seen it?"

"Might have."

"What do you mean?"

"Just what I said. Maybe I have, and maybe I haven't."

I gave up on the cook. I asked a couple of the kitchen hands about the ghost. Then I asked two of the housekeepers. I got the same sorts of answers from everyone.

Hmm. What a puzzle. This sure was interesting. Everyone seemed to be covering up when it came to the ghost story. I moved my stack of books from the library to the common room. Boy, did I have something to write about. I opened my notebook to a clean piece of paper. And after much thought I wrote:

My dearest Logan,
You can't possibly know how much I miss you. My thoughts are with you and only you every second of every day. During the night, you fill my dreams. I cannot bear to be apart from you.

I paused in my writing. I was picturing Logan on a beach in Aruba, lying on a towel next to some gorgeous girl — a girl who wasn't shy and who was good in gym. With great difficulty, I managed to finish the letter. It was six pages long. The entire last page consisted of xxx's and ooo's. I wondered if it would reach Aruba before the Brunos left, decided that it wouldn't, and didn't mail it.

I also didn't write a word of my history project.

CHAPTER 7

Jessi

Tuesday

Today went a little differently than I'd thought it would. Right up until this morning, I'd been pretty sure I'd spend it learning to ski or practicing my skating. Instead, I wound up watching Pinky Winkler. To be honest, I didn't exactly wind up watching her. I sort of volunteered for the job....

When I woke up this morning, I was so excited . . . once I got over the shock of actually waking up, that is. We (the BSC members and the Conway Cove kids) were still pretty zonked from the excitement of the night before. But when I looked out the window and saw the snow, and later when I walked into the dining hall and smelled the toast and eggs and other good breakfast smells, I felt my energy return.

Kristy sat at our table, talking a mile a minute about the activities for the day: "Since it's still snowing, we'll have ski practice first," she said. "That'll give the lodge people time to clear the snow off the pond. We'll go skating in the afternoon if we can."

"Can *we* learn to ski?" asked Amber, one of the littlest kids.

"Sure. There's a snowbunny trail especially for you guys, and a really nice instructor who'll show you what to do. Plus, Ms. Halliday will help you out."

"Ooh, I can't wait!" exclaimed Ginnie. "I have never, ever been skiing."

"I went once," spoke up Joey. Joey had this straight brown hair with a big cowlick in the front. His bottom middle teeth were missing, and so was a side one on top. "It was fun. But I fell down a lot."

Kristy grinned. Then she looked around at us BSC members. "Who else is coming to practice?" she asked.

"Me," said Stacey and Claudia at once.

"I'll come," added Dawn.

Kristy looked at Mary Anne.

"Me?" squeaked Mary Anne. "You must be kidding. No way."

"Mal?" said Kristy.

Mallory shook her head. "I'm no good on skis. I'll be in the snowball fight, though, and Jessi and I have a good idea for a snow sculpture."

"Great," said Kristy. She turned to me. "Jessi? Skiing?"

I was all set to say, "Sure. Why not? I'd like to learn." But something stopped me. It was the image of myself dancing on stage. First I saw myself in *Coppélia*, then in *Swan Lake*. I saw myself whirling around and around and . . . falling! A huge cast was on my leg and I was completely off balance.

How could I have been so stupid? I thought. I can't go skiing. I'm a dancer. I could break an arm or a leg. Come to think of it, I couldn't very well go skating, either. What if I broke

Jessi

an ankle? Suddenly even the snowball fight didn't seem too safe. Suppose I got frostbitten and had to have my toes removed. I couldn't dance without my toes. I need them for balance.

"Um," I said, stalling for time. "Um, I think I'll skip ski practice. Someone has to . . . has to watch Pinky. Yeah, that's it. Because Miss Weber and Mr. Dougherty aren't back from the hospital yet."

"Oh, I can watch her," Mary Anne told me. "I'm just going to stay inside and work on my project."

"No, no, no," I said quickly. "That's okay. You'll need to concentrate. I better stick with Pinky. We'll have lots of fun, won't we, Pinky?"

"It'll be swell," said Pinky dispiritedly.

I cringed slightly, remembering that none of the little kids had wanted Pinky for their bunkie. What was wrong with her? I wondered. Oh, well. I couldn't worry about that. I needed an excuse, and Pinky was a good one.

"Well . . . okay," said Kristy. She pushed her plate away. "Come on, everyone. Let's get going!"

Kids and teachers were starting to file out of the dining hall, so we followed them. Mal

70

and I walked on either side of Pinky, acting as crutches so that she could keep her injured foot off the ground. When we got to the common room, Mal said, "I better go. I'm working on my special project today."

"Oh, all right," I replied, suddenly dismayed at having volunteered to entertain Pinky until Miss Weber and Mr. Dougherty returned.

Pinky and I sat on opposite sides of a game table, Pinky's foot stretched out on a chair.

We looked at each other.

"I'm Jessi," I said, just in case Pinky hadn't learned all our names yet.

"I know."

"Is Pinky your real name," I asked her, "or a nickname?"

Pinky made a face. "Of course it's a nick-name," she replied. "What'd you think? My parents wouldn't be stupid enough to give me a name like Pinky."

Sheesh. I was just trying to make conversation. "What's your real name then?" I asked.

"Priscilla."

"I like Pinky better," I told her.

"I don't."

Whoa. This was one bratty little kid. No wonder none of the other children had wanted her for a bunkie.

"So how many books did you read in the readathon at your school?" I asked.

"Why do you want to know?"

"I'm *curious*," I answered, trying not to lose my temper.

Pinky sighed deeply. "Sixty-two."

"Wow! That must be some kind of record. You must really like to read."

"Duh."

I had no answer for "duh," so I kept my mouth shut.

"You know what I *don't* like?" said Pinky.

"I don't like nosy people who ask a bunch of questions. So quit asking so many questions. In fact, quit talking to me."

Quit talking to her? Now who did that remind me of? Oh, yes. The woman across the street from us in Stoneybrook. She will not allow her daughter, who's only a little younger than my sister, Becca, to talk to me or Becca or anyone in our family — because we're black. She's even threatened to move out of her house, saying that a black family in the neighborhood makes the property values on all the houses go down. She says she'll have to sell quickly before her house is worthless.

I hope she leaves soon.

I eyed Pinky across the table. Was she prejudiced, too? Would she talk like this to Mal or to Kristy? I wasn't sure. What I did know was that it was my job to entertain her, and I planned to do just that. Even if it meant talking to her.

"Well," I said, getting to my feet. "I feel like a game of Candy Land or maybe Scrabble."

"Do you know how to play poker?" asked Pinky.

"No. Sorry."

"Oh. I thought you would."

"Well, I don't. How about Scrabble?"

"I guess. If we have to."

Jessi

"We don't have to do anything. But doing *some*thing beats sitting around all day."

Pinky sighed. "Okay. Let's play." She sounded as if I'd suggested scrubbing floors instead of playing a game.

The Georges keep a big collection of board games and decks of cards in a cupboard near the check-in desk. Mary Anne had shown me where it was before she began her history research in the library. (She had also shown me the library.) I opened the cupboard and found Scrabble, Monopoly, Sorry, Chutes and Ladders, Memory, Risk, and a lot of other games. I selected Scrabble and Memory, closed the cupboard, and returned to Pinky.

"Took you long enough," Pinky greeted me.

I almost said something really nasty to her, but I held my tongue. Insulting a person never helps a bad situation. Besides, Pinky's foot hurt her, and she'd had a bad scare the day before. I needed to keep things in perspective.

So all I said was, "Look. I brought two games. Have you ever played Memory?"

Pinky studied the box the game came in. "Nope," she replied.

"Which shall we play first?"

Pinky shrugged.

"Okay, if you don't care, then I'll choose," I said. "Let's play Memory."

"First get me a soda," said Pinky.

"A soda? We just finished breakfast."

"I *know*. I'm thirsty anyway. Get me a soda."

What was I — Pinky's maid? To keep her quiet, I got her a soda from a machine.

She never thanked me.

We played three games of Memory. I won every round. I have a very good memory.

But . . . "Cheater!" cried Pinky after the third round. "Dirty cheater!" She threw the cards back in the box.

Well, I did not have to sit there while Pinky called me names and ordered me around. I could keep an eye on her from a distance. I got up, marched into the library, almost bumping into Mary Anne, who was leaving with an armload of books, pulled *Matilda*, by Roald Dahl, off of the shelf of kids' books, returned to the common room, and thrust the book into Pinky's hands.

"Here," I said. "If you like to read so much, read this."

Then I sat down next to Mary Anne, who had settled herself near the fire with her books. But right away I left. Mary Anne was looking completely sappy. She was doodling her name and Logan's all over a piece of notebook paper.

So I borrowed a piece of paper and a pencil

from her and chose another seat from where I could keep an eye on Pinky. Then I began thinking up ideas for Talent Night. All morning I worked and Pinky read.

We didn't speak again until lunchtime.

CHAPTER 8

Stacey

                    Tuesday morning.
   What a morning! Here's something
for your book, Mary Anne. I met
the world's cutest guy today. His name
is Pierre. Pierre D'Amboise. His family
is French, but Pierre was born in the
U.S. and has lived here all his life. He
doesn't speak with an accent. In fact,
he admitted that he doesn't even speak
much French. Pierre has these deep
brown eyes that twinkle. I mean, they're
really sparkly. And his voice is
starting to change, which is so cool....

I could have gone on about Pierre for pages and pages, but I didn't think Mary Anne needed quite such detailed information. Besides, some of my thoughts about Pierre were personal. But before I start talking about him again, let me go back and tell you about the morning so I can explain how Pierre and I met.

It was still snowing when we woke up, and the first thing Mallory said was, "Do you really think we might get snowed — "

"Shh!" I hissed. I held my hand out to indicate that the children might overhear us. We didn't want to scare them all over again.

"Sorry," whispered Mal.

I looked outside at the snow. I happen to love snow. We didn't get all that much of it when I lived in New York City. My personal theory is that the city is too warm for snow. It's warm from body heat — millions of people live there. Plus, the sidewalks and streets are warm because so much stuff goes on underneath them — subways, underground stores and banks. That sort of thing.

There is very little hope for a blizzard in New York City.

I was kind of wishing to get snowed in at Leicester Lodge. We'd have plenty of food and supplies, so we wouldn't be in any danger.

However, I kept that thought to myself. I didn't think anyone else wanted to get snowed in.

At breakfast, Kristy announced ski practice for the morning. The snow was already letting up a little, so there was really no reason not to hit the slopes.

"Are you coming with us?" Dawn asked as she and Kristy and Claudia were getting ready for a morning on skis.

"I'd like to, but I better not," I replied. "You guys are too good for me. I'll have to stick to the beginner trails, at least at first. Plus, I offered to help Ms. Halliday keep an eye on the kids. I'm not going to take a lesson like the children are, but I think I better look in on their class from time to time. Fifteen kids who've hardly been on skis are a lot for one teacher and one instructor to handle."

"Okay," said Kristy. "Practice hard, though. The Blue Team will need you on Friday."

"Yes, General," I replied.

Everyone laughed except Kristy.

I watched Dawn, Claud, and Kristy head downstairs, Claudia lugging her ski equipment. Then I watched Mal pull her journal out from under her mattress (who was she fooling?) and leave the room with it, and I watched Mary Anne find a pad of paper and a pencil and leave with *them*. Pinky and Jessi had stayed downstairs, I knew. So it was just me, Ms. Halliday, and fifteen kids who needed to dress for snowy weather.

I swear, I have never seen so many clothes. Each kid wanted to put on (over his indoor clothes) a sweater, an extra pair of socks, plastic baggies over the sock layers to keep his feet dry inside the ski boots, two pairs of mittens, a hat, a scarf, and a snowsuit (and boy, are snowsuits complicated things — zippers, buttons, buckles, and snaps everywhere).

It took us a full half hour to get those kids dressed, and wouldn't you know it, no sooner did we think we'd finished than we started hearing things like:

"Stacey? I have to go to the bathroom."

"Me, too."

"Me, too."

"Stacey, I put my snowsuit on, but I forgot my sweater."

"Me, too."

"Bryce, cut it out, you sorehead!" (That was Joey. I'm not sure what he and Bryce were arguing about.)

"Stacey, my mittens don't match."

"Neither do mine."

After another fifteen or twenty minutes we were ready to go.

Sort of.

Have you ever tried to fit fifteen children for skis, boots, and poles?

Probably not. I hadn't.

I guess you can imagine, though, that it took nearly forever, and I am not exaggerating. By the time the kids were *finally* ready, and Ms. Halliday and I had our skis, too, I could not wait for a run down one of the beginner trails. But I knew I ought to help the kids get organized in their class, even though Ms. Halliday kept saying, "Go on, Stacey. I've got things under control."

At last I took her advice. I rode the ski lift to the top of one of the beginner trails. A baby trail, Kristy would call it, but I prefer to say "beginner trail."

I managed to get off the lift without falling, to turn around, and to head slowly down the slope. I tried to remember the few things I'd learned from the lessons I'd taken. I couldn't remember much, but at least I arrived at the bottom of the trail in one piece — which is more than I can say for Mr. Show-off, Alan Gray, alias Kristy's Nemesis. He tried to do all this fancy stuff and landed at the end of the trail on his bottom with one leg in front of him, the other behind, and his poles lying about ten feet away. He wasn't hurt, but he caused three other boys to crash into him, and a fourth to fall over one of his poles.

I shook my head and got on the ski lift again. Then I began my descent to the end of the trail, only this time I picked up speed. I could see that Alan and his pals had cleared away from the scene of their accident. Good, I thought, and skied happily until I realized that someone was right behind me and staying there.

I was being tailgated on skis.

"Alan, cut it out!" I yelled into the wind and snow. I was afraid to turn around, though. I was sure I'd lose my balance.

By the time we reached the bottom of the trail, I was completely unnerved. "Cut it *out!*" I yelled again. Only this time I did turn around, and of course I fell.

Someone fell on top of me.

I looked over my shoulder and right into the eyes of . . . a gorgeous guy.

It wasn't Alan at all.

"Oh, no!" I cried. "I'm so sorry!"

"Don't be," said the boy. "It wasn't your fault. It was mine. I don't have very good control over these skis yet. I knew I was on your tail, but I couldn't help it."

"Well, that's okay." I was all out of breath. And I couldn't tell if it was because of our accident, or because of the amazing face I was gazing at.

Somehow, the two of us managed to untangle ourselves and stand up. As soon as we did, we fell again. We burst out laughing.

"This is like a Laurel and Hardy movie," said the boy.

"Or a *Three Stooges* show," I added. I had to stop laughing so I could catch my breath.

When we were on our feet and had calmed

down, the boy said, "My name's Pierre. Pierre D'Amboise."

"I'm Stacey McGill," I told him.

Here is a fact: It is very difficult to shake hands when you're wearing ski mittens. They're so puffy and fat it's like shaking hands with giant marshmallows.

"Where are you from?" Pierre asked me as we panted our way to the ski lift.

"Stoneybrook, Connecticut," I answered. "My whole school is here. I'm in eighth grade."

"I'm in eighth, too," said Pierre. "My class is here for the week. We're from Dixville Falls. That's upstate. Almost in Canada."

"Wow," I said. "Canada. Are you French Canadian? I mean, is your family French Canadian?"

"Nope. We're French French. My parents grew up in Paris, but right after they got married, they moved to the States. I've always lived in Vermont. I barely speak French, and I take Italian in school. I am a real embarrassment to my parents."

I laughed. "Do you speak *any* French?"

"Chevrolet coupé."

That time I laughed so hard I nearly fell over. Ski boots tip you forward, and it is not easy to laugh all tipped over on skis in slippery snow.

Pierre caught me by the arm and kept me upright. "Come on," he said. "It's our turn."

We were at the head of the line for the ski lift, and we let ourselves be scooped up and carried to the top of the trail. Then we skied down together. Or sort of together, since neither of us is great. At least we didn't crash into each other at the bottom.

Much as I wanted to make another run with Pierre, I knew that it was time for me to check on Ms. Halliday and the kids. I explained to Pierre what I had to do, and then I set off for the snowbunny group. When I reached it, I found fifteen exuberant children, most of whom were sure they were just about ready to enter the next Winter Olympics.

"How's everything going?" I asked Ms. Halliday.

"Oh, just fine," she replied. "The kids are great. So enthusiastic."

"No problems?"

"Nope. The instructor's great, too."

"Okay. Do you mind if I go back to the trails? I want to, um, practice some more."

"Go ahead. We're doing fine here."

"Thanks, Ms. Halliday!" I called as I made

my way back to the ski lift. All I could think about as I struggled along was Pierre.

Pierre D'Amboise. The name alone made me feel ultrasophisticated, almost continental. I pictured Pierre's sparkling eyes, his brown hair with the streaks of blond in it. (Had he been out in the sun recently? On some faraway island, perhaps?) Then I remembered his voice. It was changing, acquiring that deepness.

I thought over the other boys I've known — the boys at school, the boys I'd met at the Sea City beach. And I decided that Pierre was the nicest, the most fun, and — if things went my way — probably my first meaningful crush. Any past crushes suddenly didn't count.

CHAPTER 9

Mallory

☺

Wednesday morning

Hi, Mary Anne. I hope it's okay if I
take my notes for you right out of my journal,
because that's what I'm doing. Okay, here's
what happened today:

Wednesday started with an awful
announcement at breakfast. Our vice-
principal made it. He stood up and said
in this cheery voice, "SMS students, I am
pleased to announce that this year, on
Friday night, an all-school dance will be
held in the lodge's grand ballroom. The
dance will be hosted by the Georges for
all students here at the lodge. You'll have
a chance to meet some new people, but
mostly to wind up your week in Hooksett
Crossing with an evening of fun."

Fun? Was he kidding? Oh, horrors.
Friday was going to be the worst night
of my life....

Here is the thing about dances: I hate them. Well, no, that's not quite true. It's more like I'm afraid of them. Actually, it's more like I'm afraid of dancing and of boys. See, I don't know how to dance. And I hardly ever spend time with boys except my brothers and boys that I baby-sit for, and they don't count. Not in the Game of Boys.

When the vice-principal made that announcement I thought I was going to faint right in the middle of the dining hall. Before he had even finished speaking I had grown so pale that Jessi had leaned over, put her hand on my arm, and exclaimed in a loud whisper, "Mal! Are you okay?"

I swallowed a couple of times. "Yes. I'll be fine," I replied, but my voice came out sounding choked up.

"Are you sure?" asked Jessi. "What's the matter?"

"Nothing," I whispered.

Oh, no. A dance. A *dance*. I couldn't think of worse news. Well, a blizzard might be worse. Getting snowed into a building with Alan "Show-off" Gray would definitely be worse. But an all-school dance was right up there on the list of things I did not want.

Right away I began to think of ways to get

out of going. Maybe the dance wasn't mandatory. If it wasn't, I could hide out somewhere and write in my journal or read. If it was, well . . . maybe I could pretend to be sick. Come to think of it, I probably wouldn't have to do much pretending. Just thinking of the dance made me pretty sick.

I looked around our breakfast table. There were the sixteen children. Pinky's bandage had been removed, and her foot was better, although not as strong as the doctor had hoped, so he had said she could walk on her foot, but couldn't go skiing or skating until the next day. And Miss Weber and Mr. Dougherty were back. Miss Weber's arm was in a cast and sling, and Mr. Dougherty's ribs were taped up. You couldn't see that, of course. The only sign of his injuries was the slow, painful way in which he walked. Neither teacher was in tip-top shape.

Scattered among the children were Ms. Halliday and my friends. I noticed that Mary Anne was sitting as far from Ms. Halliday as she could get. Across from me was Jessi. We needed to talk about our snow sculpture, since the contest was that afternoon. Before we'd left Stoneybrook, Jessi had been gung-ho over the project. (We had planned to sculpt a pair of ballet slippers with feet in them.) Now, every time I mentioned the contest, Jessi began to talk about things like frostbite and her toes and her dancing career. Further down the table, Claudia and Stacey were having a heavy conference about something, and Dawn was trying to get Pinky to finish her breakfast.

Kristy, sitting near the middle of the table next to Ms. Halliday, stood up and tapped her knife on her glass of orange juice.

"Attention!" she called. "Can I have your attention?"

The dining hall quieted down — but not enough, so Kristy handed the knife to Ms. Halliday, who tapped for her, while Kristy stood up on her chair.

"ATTENTION!" she called.

Since it was the second announcement of the meal, no one was too eager to stop talking.

But when Kristy finally yelled, *"ATTEN-TION, PLEASE!"* the room grew silent. "Thank you," said Kristy. "I want to announce that the ice-skating contest will be held this morning. It will begin at ten-thirty. If you want to participate, please show up at the pond about fifteen minutes early. The snow-sculpture contest will be held in the afternoon. Please arrive by two-fifteen so we can start at two-thirty. The contest will take place on the lawn in front of the lodge. One last thing. The skiing events will be held on Friday. Remember that you can take free lessons from the instructors here. If you don't want lessons, then practice, practice, practice, okay?"

"Okay!" replied a few kids.

Kristy sat down, looking flushed. She certainly was taking her job seriously.

"Well," Jessi said to me, "what are you going to do this morning?"

"I'm not sure. What are you going to do?"

"Work on the talent sh — Oh, that reminds me. I've got to make an announcement, too."

As you can probably guess, it took even longer for Jessi to get everyone's attention than it had taken Kristy. In fact, Ms. Halliday had to blow her gym whistle to make us quiet down. At last Jessi, who stood on her chair like Kristy in order to be heard, said, "Sorry to interrupt you again, but I want to announce that auditions for the talent show will be held in the grand ballroom this afternoon as soon as the snow-sculpture contest is over. If you want to be in the show but don't know what to do, come to the auditions anyway, because I have some ideas. Thank you."

Jessi sat down. The vice-principal stood up. "I would like to announce," he said, "that there will be no further announcements."

Everyone cheered. And then people began

to leave the dining hall. I was on my own for the morning. Jessi had her work to do. Kristy, Claudia, and Dawn were going to be in the ice-skating contest, Mary Anne was busy moping and working on *her* project, and Stacey seemed to be in an awful rush to get somewhere. Where? I wondered.

Then I remembered my *own* project. I tore up to our dorm, slipped my journal out of its hiding place under my mattress, and took it down to the common room to write about the events of the morning.

This was my journal project: I planned to work hard on my writing, since I want to become an author one day. A big place with a lot of new people and activities was perfect for honing my observational skills. I planned to play Harriet from *Harriet the Spy*, just like I'd done when my friends and I went on this cruise to the Bahamas and then traveled to Disney World. Only I intended to be a better spy than Harriet. For one thing, I was not going to get caught. For another, I was going to be such a keen observer that my journal would be filled only with the truth. I would never, ever read something into a situation that wasn't really there.

For awhile, I just sat in the common room and wrote about my feelings and reactions to what had gone on so far that morning. I started off with:

The children are in very good moods today, except for Pinky, who is mad that she can't go skiing or skating until tomorrow. I'm really surprised at how quickly the kids bounced back from the bus catastrophe. My mom once said that children are resilient. She should know, since she's got eight of them.

Then I began observing what was going on in the common room:

Mary Anne is all broken up over Logan. I'm pretty sure about this because I peeked at what she was writing, and instead of filling her pages with information about Hooksett Crossing and Leicester Lodge, she's writing things like:

Mary Anne and Logan   Mary Anne Bruno
Mrs. L. Bruno   Logan Spier (hmm...)
Mary Anne Spier-Bruno XXX, OOO
♡♡♡ Logan, my love, my one and only ♡♡♡

Every now and then she gets hold of herself and writes about her project, but not very often. From what I can see of her notes, this lodge is haunted! I never knew that before. But maybe that explains the white thing I saw in the corner of our dorm last night. Then again, it might just have been Stacey's bathrobe, hanging on a hook.

When I got bored with the common room, I decided to try some hard-core spying. I carried my notebook into the dining hall. It was empty of people (of course), and so big that my footsteps echoed, so I had to tiptoe. Cautiously, I approached the kitchen. Swinging double doors lead into it and one door was propped open. I peeped around it and saw several of the cook's helpers preparing lunch. Then I saw the cook himself. He's this old guy with not much hair, a stubbly beard, and one top tooth missing. Up until now I'd thought he'd seemed really nice. But when I peeked in at him, this is what was going on:

The cook is sprinkling something into a vat of soup. The stuff is coming from a jar that's not labeled. I think it is poison. And now he's picking up a huge knife. Oh, no. The cook is crazy. He may be trying to kill us all!

I fled back to the common room, where Pinky, Joey, Ginnie, and Bryce were playing a silly board game called Operation. Ginnie and Joey were yelling at Pinky and she was having a temper tantrum. I have a feeling Pinky isn't too popular.

By this time I had to go to the bathroom. I used the ladies' room downstairs, and who should I see in there, but Ms. Halliday. And she was crying:

I know Ms. Halliday is crying, even though she's trying to cover it up. She keeps dabbing at her eyes with a wet paper towel and saying, "Isn't this silly? I've worn contacts for years and they still give me trouble."

But I know better. Ms. Halliday's contacts aren't bothering her. She's suffering from unrequited love. She has a crush on the vice-principal, but he isn't interested in her. Guess who else has a crush on someone? Stacey. She likes a boy! I saw them kissing!!

Boy, was my journal ever juicy. I would have to find a better hiding place for it than under my mattress. At home, too. If my little brothers or sisters ever found this, they would read things that are *far* too mature for them.

CHAPTER 10

Dawn

Wednesday morning
Here are my notes, Mary
Anne. I'm being as honest
as possible, but I hope
you don't put everything
I write into your book for
Logan. Some of this stuff
is embarrassing. He doesn't
really need to know all of it,
so use your good judgment
and take out the worst stuff,
okay?
This was not a good day
for me, as you well know,
since you were part of the
problem. (No offense. Just
being honest. That's what

you asked for.) Anyway, the ice-skating competition was a disaster. I am so humiliated....

When we woke up on Wednesday it was still snowing — not hard, just enough to make Kristy crazy.

"How can we hold the sculpture contest this afternoon?" she cried. "The snow will just keep covering up everyone's work. It'll be a disaster."

"Why don't you wait until this afternoon to decide whether to call off the contest?" Ms. Halliday suggested at breakfast. "It's barely snowing, Kristy. I think you should announce the contest anyway. If you have to call it off — and I doubt you will — you can announce the change in schedule at lunchtime. Right now, the snow seems to be letting up."

So Kristy made her announcements. As soon as breakfast was over, she and Claud and I got our skates and headed for the pond so that we could practice before the contest began. We found pretty many other kids there, too. I'm no great skater, but I'm not bad. I practiced skating fast, skating backward, and making figure eights. That's about the best I can do.

There were to be three parts to the contest. The first part was speed. Each person on each team would be clocked to see how fast he or she could skate fifty yards. It was the skating version of the fifty-yard dash. The team with the fastest skater would earn one point. Next was a sort of relay race. The teams would divide in two, half of each team standing on one side of the pond, the other halves across from them. Then we were given ten minutes in which to see how many times the members of each team could carry a baton back and forth across the ice. If everyone on a team went once before the time was up, they just started over. That's why it didn't matter whether the Red and the Blue Teams were evenly represented. Again, the team that made the most trips across the pond earned a point. The tiebreaker event (if it was needed) was a sort of obstacle course. Ten members from each team were selected to do the following: skate backward to the middle of the pond, execute a figure eight, then continue to the opposite side, skating in and out of a row of coffee cans. The team that finished first won a point, and the team that earned two out of three points was the overall winner of the competition.

Kristy got things rolling promptly at ten-thirty.

"All right, teams," she said, facing the kids who had gathered. (Thirty-one Red Team members and twenty-eight Blue Team members were there.) "Our first event is speed skating. Every one of you may participate."

Kristy went on to explain the rules. Then she organized us into two long lines, handed a stopwatch to Mr. Cheney, the scorekeeper, and took her place at the head of the line of Blue Team members. Rick Chow stood at the head of the Red Team line. Mr. Cheney tossed a coin, and our team, the Blue Team, won the right to go first.

So Kristy sailed across the ice to the flag that had been placed fifty yards out on the pond. For someone short, she sure is fast. She made excellent time. Then Rick Chow took his turn. He was not as fast as Kristy.

You might think that watching fifty-nine kids skate out to a flag one at a time would get boring after awhile, but it didn't. We just kept cheering and cheering. And each time someone would beat the best score, Mr. Cheney would call out the new time. It was pretty exciting.

I waited nervously for my turn, my heart pumping, and the adrenaline flowing through my body. I concentrated so hard on that flag across the ice that Mr. Cheney had to say, "Take your mark, get set, go!" three times before I heard him. Then I went whizzing off — and halfway to the flag I hit a bump on the ice, tripped, and fell. I knew I had to get up and keep going, so I did. I also knew I had just contributed the slowest time so far to our team.

I was right.

But our team won anyway. This girl named Andrea Kirkland had the fastest time.

As we were gearing up for the relay race, Kristy thumped me on the back, said not to worry, and wished me better luck in the next event. I felt relieved — until I saw two seventh-graders from the other team pointing at me and laughing.

I ignored them. Mom says I'm like a duck in a storm. Insults roll right off my back like raindrops off a duck's feathers. I geared myself up for the relay race, giving myself a silent pep talk.

The race began. The cheering was loud and constant since the skaters on both teams kept going and going at the same time. When Paul Friedman finally slapped the baton into my hand — I dropped it! My mittens were so fat and clumsy. But I picked it right up and skated out across the ice. This time I don't know how I fell, but I did. One second I was skating along, the next second I was on my hands and knees. It took me awhile to get up and find the baton. I lost a lot of time for my team.

And the Red Team won. Now we would have to hold the tiebreaker event.

"Teams!" Kristy cried, standing in front of us participants. "Get ready for the tiebreaker. I want each team captain — that's you and me, Rick — "

("Duh," said Rick under his breath.)

" — to select ten kids to participate in this, the final event."

We divided into teams and Kristy looked over the kids on our team. Then she carefully selected ten people.

I was not one of them.

I watched the tiebreaker silently, unable to cheer. I just didn't have any cheers in me. When our team finally lost the ice-skating competition, two kids actually came up to me and said sarcastically, "Nice going, Dawn."

My cheeks began to burn. Why were they insulting me? Anyone could fall . . . twice . . . and drop the baton.

I was about to go back to our dorm for awhile when Kristy announced practice for the snowball fight. Considering what had happened when I tried to ice-skate, I decided I better not miss a practice. So I went.

The mock fight took place at the edge of some woods not far from the skating pond. The first thing that happened when it began was that Alan Gray hit me in the face with a snowball and then stuffed another one down the back of my ski jacket.

"Ha, ha!" he sang. "Ha, ha. Ha, ha-ha, ha, ha!"

I can't stand when people do that. Furthermore, a bunch of other kids had seen what

Alan had done. They were laughing, too. I was surrounded by ha-has. I needed to escape. So I simply left the fight. Since there was still some time before lunch, I decided to get a pair of boots and skis and take a couple of runs down the mountain to clear my head and drive away some of the anger I could feel building up.

I'm a pretty good skier (yes, you can ski in California, plus Dad took us to Vail, Colorado, a couple of times), so I headed for the intermediate trails, expecting to go on the advanced ones later that afternoon.

But I didn't get any further than the ski lift. I fell trying to get *on* it. (Most people, if they're going to fall, fall getting off.) The kids in line behind me snickered.

Okay. Enough was enough. Usually I don't care what anyone says or thinks about me, but one too many people had laughed at me that morning. In a huff, I returned the boots, skis, and poles, and marched back to the lodge. I stomped into the common room and right over to Mary Anne, who was writing in that book for Logan.

"Well, congratulate me," I said.

Mary Anne looked up, blinking her eyes. "Huh?"

"Congratulate me."

104

"For what?"

"For walking from the ski rental office to the lodge without falling down."

Mary Anne paused. At last she said, "I'm not — Did you have a bad morning or something?"

"Yes, I had a bad morning." I flumped into an armchair next to Mary Anne.

"What happened?"

I gave Mary Anne the grisly details — from falling on the ice to falling off the ski lift. I waited expectantly for the sympathy to come pouring out, since Mary Anne is the most sensitive, caring person I know, and also, with a little luck, will be my future stepsister.

But the words that came out of Mary Anne's mouth were, "Do you have any idea how far Aruba is from Hooksett Crossing?"

My jaw must have dropped because Mary Anne immediately said "What? What's wrong?"

"What's wrong?" I exploded. "I'm sitting here pouring out my heart to you — which, by the way, I don't do very often — and all you can think of is your precious Logan. Have you thought of anything or anyone else since we left Stoneybrook?"

Mary Anne narrowed her eyes at me. She doesn't lose her temper often, but she's human, after all. She just has a longer-than-usual, very slow-burning fuse. I had a feeling I'd reached the end of it.

I was right.

POW!

Mary Anne let loose. "Of *course* I've thought of other things," she cried. "I've been working on my project . . . sort of . . . and rescuing children, and — "

"Oh, forget it," I snapped. "You still didn't hear a word I said. And friends are supposed to listen when they're needed."

"Then I guess I'm not much of a friend, am I?"

"I guess not."

"Fine."

"You're fired as my bunkie."

"You can't fire me, because I fire you."

Well, it didn't matter who fired whom. All I know is that I stomped up to our dorm, yanked the blankets and sheets off my bed, and made up the empty bed on the bunk beneath Pinky's.

I decided that I was not speaking to Ms. Mary Anne Spier, my ex-bunkie and former friend.

CHAPTER 11

Mary Anne

Wednesday afternoon

Ooh, I am so mad at Dawn Schafer. Logan, you should have heard her this morning. I don't know what got into her. She had a bad day and she took it out on me. Not only is that unlike Dawn, but it wasn't fair. If she wants someone to listen to her so much, she should get a dog. Or a parrot, so it could talk back to her. Well, maybe that's not fair, either. Maybe I should have listened to her. I'm her best friend, after all. On the other hand, I was having problems of my own. Not serious ones. I mean, not too serious. Oh, I don't know....

Wednesday was not the best day of my week at the lodge, although it started off okay. After breakfast I decided to interview three of the old-time lodge employees. One was Marie Castleman, the head housekeeper, who was at least seventy-five years old; one was Teensy Mooseman, who's real name is Rebeccah, but no one calls her that, and who was in charge of all the gardeners and handymen, and who was also about seventy-five; and the last one was Curtis Oates, the head cook, who looked a little younger than Marie and Teensy — maybe seventy or so.

I started with Marie, mostly because as I was leaving the library, I passed her office and saw her in there.

"Excuse me," I said, knocking lightly on the doorjamb.

Marie looked up. "Yes?" Her gray hair was frazzly, she wore gold-rimmed granny glasses, and she was as skinny as a wet cat. But what I couldn't help noticing first were her ears. They were pierced, and must have been pierced for decades, and Marie must have worn very heavy earrings in them for all those decades because now her earlobes were, well, let's just say droopy.

"Um, hi, I'm Mary Anne Spier," I said. "I'm

writing a paper about Hooksett Crossing and Leicester Lodge, and Mrs. George said you've worked here for a long time and — "

"Only since nineteen-thirty," Marie interrupted proudly.

"Since nineteen-thirty. Wow!"

Marie smiled. She rested her pen in a holder and gestured for me to come in and sit down. I did, and right away she began talking, so I began taking notes. "The lodge was only ten years old when I began working here," she said. "The Georges didn't own it yet, of course. They weren't even born yet. And the lodge was nowhere near this size. Huge additions were built in the forties and fifties."

I let Marie talk for almost fifteen minutes before I said, "I heard the lodge has a ghost."

Silence.

"I — I read that in Mr. George's book," I ventured.

Marie sniffed. "I don't hold store by such things."

"But have you ever seen a ghost here? Or anything weird?"

"Never. Not once," Marie replied quickly.

I nodded. "Well, thank you very much. I really appreciate your talking to me. It was a big help."

"Any time." Marie smiled again. Was it a

smile of relief? I wondered. A smile because I hadn't pressed the ghost issue?

I found Curtis Oates in the kitchen, showing a new cook how to make tuna salad for eight hundred. When I saw that he was busy, I started to back out of the double doors, but Curtis looked up and smiled. He is missing a tooth, which is something I just can't stand. I mean, in adults. I am a firm believer in dentures.

"Well," I said, "I wanted to interview you for my paper on Hooksett Crossing and the lodge, but you're busy, so I'll come back later."

"Oh, now hold on," Curtis replied. "I'm at a good stopping place. I was just getting ready to take a coffee break. Do you drink coffee?"

"Uh, no. Thanks." I tried to picture the look on my father's face if he were to catch me drinking coffee. He has often said that coffee will prevent me from growing — and I am not that tall to begin with.

Curtis poured himself a cup of coffee and we sat across from each other at a butcher-block table where someone had been chopping onions. The onions made my eyes run, but they didn't seem to effect Curtis.

I asked Curtis what Hooksett Crossing had been like when he was a boy, and he told me all about it and also how the town had changed during the Depression, and again during World War II. Then he told me how the Georges had come to buy the lodge in 1963. Finally I asked my big question — what about the ghost?

Curtis suddenly lost the power of speech. He became as unresponsive as when I'd asked him about the ghost the last time. So I thanked him (with onion tears welling up in my eyes), and went off in search of Teensy Mooseman.

Teensy is not too hard to find in the wintertime, since there isn't a lot of gardening and grounds work to be done. I headed for the boiler room, because, according to Mrs. George, the boiler breaks down with great regularity all winter long. Sure enough, there was Teensy and two repair people. Despite her age, Teensy was wearing blue jean overalls, a plaid shirt, and a paint-spattered baseball cap.

Teensy was just as eager to talk as Marie and Curtis had been — until I pulled out the ghost question. Then she clammed up. All I could get out of her was, "No such things as ghosts." (Actually, she said, "No setch things as ghosts.") This was getting me nowhere. And the more people avoided the ghost subject, the more I wanted to hear about it.

I decided I should talk to Mr. George, since

he'd devoted three chapters in his book to the ghost. And Mr. George did turn out to be helpful. At least he would talk.

"The ghost story," he said, "seems to have stemmed from the death of a visitor to the lodge in the late nineteen-thirties. One morning he was found dead in his bathtub. No one knew what had happened to him. But when his relatives heard the news, they seemed awfully relieved. They seemed to think he was evil. One went so far as to say he was in league with the devil. And none of them would agree to take his body away for burial, so he was buried in the woods here. The owner of the lodge took pity on the dead man. But as soon as he'd been laid to rest, visitors and workers here began reporting odd occurrences."

"Like what?" I asked.

"Oh, the usual. Nothing they couldn't have read in a mystery book — windows that opened themselves on rainy nights, vague white figures drifting down dark hallways or staircases," (I shivered) "odd moaning noises, also usually at night. That sort of thing."

"And what do you think?" I asked.

"I think," Mr. George answered with a smile, "that my wife and I have owned the lodge for over twenty years and haven't experienced *any* of those things. Not one. A few of our guests have. And Curtis had quite a scare one night, but we think people's imaginations tend to run away with them. Period."

I asked what kind of scare Curtis had had, and Mr. George said something about his mistaking a pile of laundry for a ghost. Not too interesting. So I returned to the common room and started to write up the notes from my interviews. I couldn't concentrate, though. No matter how hard I tried to work, I kept finding myself picturing Logan and that gorgeous girl doing all sorts of island things together —

snorkeling, waterskiing, tanning . . . kissing.

A horrible feeling settled in the pit of my stomach. And just when the feeling was at its worst, Dawn returned to the lodge, slumped into a chair, and picked a fight with me. Honest. She really did. She accused me of being insensitive, and then she fired me as her bunkie and moved all her stuff to the empty bed under Pinky's.

What a baby. Why did I ever think she was one of my best friends?

When Dawn huffed off, I moved to one of two chairs hidden in a corner of the common room. They were facing out a window, which meant their backs were to the rest of the room. Perfect. I didn't feel like looking at anyone or talking to anybody.

Once again, I tried to work. I had written exactly three sentences when someone sat down in the chair next to me. For a long time, I managed not to look over at the person. I wanted to be alone, and I hoped that whoever it was would go away.

But the person didn't leave. However, he (or she) didn't speak to me, either. And after awhile I became so curious about this quiet person who was probably as depressed as I was that I just had to look over and see who it was.

114

When I did, I saw . . . dum da-dum dum . . . Ms. Halliday.

Yikes!

I started to leave, realizing that Ms. Halliday didn't even know I was there. Or if she did, she didn't care. She looked as pensive and as sad as I probably looked.

As quietly as I could, I gathered up my things. I was just starting to tiptoe away, when . . . dum da-dum-dum . . . Ms. Halliday *spoke to me*.

"You don't have to leave," she said.

"Oh, that's okay. I was just . . . just . . ." What *was* I doing? Escaping?

"You look pretty sad," Ms. Halliday observed.

"So do you," I couldn't help replying.

"I miss someone," Ms. Halliday said simply.

"Me, too," I whispered.

"Really? Who?"

This didn't sound like the screaming gym teacher I remembered, so I told her about Logan. Then *she* told me about her fiancé. He was a reporter for our Stoneybrook newspaper, and boy, did she ever miss him. It turned out that they'd never been separated for more than a couple of days.

I must have had a funny look on my face because after a pause, Ms. Halliday said, "You know, Mary Anne, I have a feeling that you think I don't like you."

I was completely taken aback, but this quiet Ms. Halliday seemed pretty easy to talk to, so I found the courage to say, "That's . . . that's true. I'm so bad at sports. I know I was a really frustrating gym student. I guess I do think you don't like me. Actually, I think you hate me."

"Oh, Mary Anne, no. I'm sorry. I pushed you last year, that's for sure, because I wanted you to try your hardest. But I know that not everyone is a born athlete. In fact, I admired you because you kept trying. Even when I asked you to do difficult things."

Really? Wow! I felt a whole lot better — about everything, even my fight with Dawn. I knew we'd make up sooner or later. And when Jessi asked me if I'd help the little kids plan a skit for the talent show, I said yes right away.

The day was looking brighter.

CHAPTER 12

Kristy

Wednesday

Sorry, Mary Anne, but I don't have time to write much for you. I'm too busy with the Winter War. This morning we held the ice-skating competition, then I started a practice snowball fight, and while that was going on, I organized a snowman-building contest for the Conway Cove kids. They needed something special to do. This afternoon is the snow-sculpture competition, then more ski practice.

Gotta go. 'Bye!

Whew! Tuesday was easy compared to Wednesday. With the Winter War underway I was running around like a chicken with its head cut off. (I know that's a disgusting analogy but my stepfather says it all the time.)

The first event of the day was the skating contest, which my team *lost*. I had fully expected to win. There were some really good athletes on my team, but darn old Dawn was being a total klutz. I didn't know she was such a klutz. If I *had* known, I wouldn't have encouraged her to enter the contests. And I was certainly going to quit asking Mary Anne to participate. We did not need another klutz. I know that sounds mean but, well, I wanted to *win*. I was the team captain and I like winning, okay? What's wrong with that?

As I said in my notes for Mary Anne's book, after we lost the ice-skating event, I started a snowball fight so the kids could practice for the real thing the next day. Once that was underway, I rounded up the Conway Cove kids and asked them if they wanted to have a snowman-building competition. Nine of them did, so I set them up in an area on the front lawn near where the snow sculptures would be built in the afternoon.

I should mention here that it had *finally*

stopped snowing. I should also mention that the sky was darker than it had been when we'd woken up in the morning, and guess what the weather report called for: a ripsnorter of a storm (I got the weather report from Teensy Mooseman) that was supposed to move in late Thursday night.

Anyway, here are the kids who wanted to build snowmen: Renée, Corey, Kara, Valerie, Frankie, Ian, Amber, Ryan, and Kathie. Bryce, Joey, Ginnie, and Pinky were playing inside, and the others were off skiing.

I needed someone to help me with this last-minute contest, and it wasn't easy tracking down a BSC member who was free. Jessi, Mal, and Mary Anne were working on their projects, Dawn had gone off angry, and Stacey was nowhere to be found. Finally I had to drag Claud away from the snowball fight.

"Come on," I said. "It'll be good practice for judging the snow sculptures this afternoon. Besides, I *really* need you. Everyone else is busy, mad at me, or has disappeared."

Reluctantly, Claudia came with me.

"All right," I said to the kids, "each of you has until fifteen minutes before lunchtime to build a snowman. You can use any props you want — scarves or hats or sticks or whatever. Claudia will choose the winning snowman."

"Snow *person*," spoke up Kara. "It doesn't have to be a man, you know."

And Frankie asked, "What does the winner get?"

Hmm. Good question. The winners of the Winter War were each going to get a coupon for a free slice of pizza at the Pizza Pan back in Stoneybrook. But what could we give the Conway Cove winner?

"I know!" Claudia cried suddenly. "But I can't tell you what it is. It'll be a surprise."

"What if we don't like it?" asked Amber.

Yeah, I thought.

But all Claud would say was, "Trust me. It's good."

So, looking dubious, the kids got to work on their snowmen. They rolled and patted the snow. Sometimes they needed help. Corey seemed to think that bigger was better and rolled three balls that were so huge and heavy he needed both Claudia and me to help him set the middle part on the bottom, and the head on the middle part.

Kara worked diligently on a snow woman who was wearing a long skirt.

And Ian made a snow Martian.

Once the bodies were built, the kids began running into the hotel for props. And Claud and I began laughing. Those kids were making really imaginative snow creatures. Valerie put glasses on hers. Renée dressed hers in Mr. Dougherty's ski jacket. Kara stuck boots under the skirt of the snow woman. Ian made tinfoil antennae for his Martian.

Fifteen minutes before lunchtime I shouted, "Time's up, you guys!"

"Oh," groaned at least half the kids.

"We're not finished," complained Ryan.

"Sorry," I replied. "Our judge needs a few minutes to make her decision. Everyone stand next to your snowma — snow creature."

Obediently, the kids stopped their work.

Claudia paced up and down in front of the nine masterpieces, her hands behind her back, her brow furrowed. She was deep in thought. Was this how she planned to look when she judged our snow sculptures?

At long last (when there were only about ten minutes left before lunch), Claudia stopped her pacing, stood beside me, and said, "I am pleased to announce that the third-place winner is Frankie and his snow farmer. The second-place winner is Ian and his snow Martian. And finally . . . the grand-prize winner is Kara and her snow woman!"

"Hurray!" cried Kara.

The other kids tried to smile, but they weren't very successful. "Now don't anyone go away," said Claud. "Wait right here for the prizes. All of you."

"What? What prizes?" asked the kids as Claud dashed inside.

"I have no idea," I replied honestly.

When Claudia returned, she was carrying her Polaroid camera. She snapped a photo of each kid with his or her creation. By the end of the day, the photos were displayed in the common room with a yellow ribbon under Frankie's picture, a red one under Ian's, and a huge blue one under Kara's. You should have seen the looks on the kids' faces when they saw the display. For the rest of the week, they kept hanging around it, especially Kara. I had to hand it to Claud. For someone who thinks she isn't smart, she sure comes up with good ideas.

By two-fifteen, when the snow-sculpture contest was getting underway, the sky was so heavy with clouds that I wouldn't have been surprised if it had fallen down, just like Chicken Little was afraid of. Of course it didn't. And the snow held off, too.

Fifteen minutes later, I found myself saying, "The snow-sculpture contest will now begin! You have an hour to work on your sculptures. The creators of the best sculpture will win this event for their team. And for those of you who don't know, the Red Team won the skating contest this morning. Okay, teams, get to work!"

All across the lawn, groups of kids began shaping mounds of snow. Very few contestants were working alone. In fact, Ashley Wyeth and a sixth-grade boy I didn't know were the only ones.

I thought the Conway Cove kids had been serious snow-person builders this morning, but I wasn't prepared for us older kids. Lots of us were equipped with buckets of water to help freeze the snow into shapes. We had no rules apart from the time limit.

I was working with Dawn and Stacey on a giant teddy bear. (Dawn was barely speaking to me.) Not far away Jessi and Mal were working on something that I couldn't identify. Good. They were on the other team. I hoped Claud wouldn't be able to identify it, either.

The hour flew by so quickly that when Claudia told me the time was up, I could hardly believe it. Then Claud began her pacing again. She and Mr. Cheney, the co-judge, examined each sculpture thoroughly. I grew extremely impatient waiting for their decision.

After what seemed like hours, Claudia said, "It wasn't easy, but we've decided that the winning sculpture is Troy Parker and Amelia White's Cheshire Cat from *Alice in Wonderland*.

Oh, brother, I should have known better than to agree to let Claud judge the contest. Of course she'd chosen a sculpture by Red Team members. My team had lost *again*. The only way we could win the Winter War now was if we beat the Red Team in every other contest.

Sheesh.

I couldn't help giving Claud a dirty look.

And I noticed that I wasn't the only one doing so. Ashley looked pretty disgusted herself. And no wonder. She *is* one of the best artists in the school, not to mention a member of the Blue Team and one of Claud's good friends. I know she had expected Claud to choose hers as the winning entry in the contest.

I sighed deeply. My team just *had* to win the war. Suddenly energized, I announced, "Don't forget ski practice, everybody. Take a lesson or just hit the slopes. You've only got until Friday to get yourselves in top form."

Then I joined Claud. "Going skiing now?" I asked her.

"I don't know. Maybe. I'm sort of tired."

"I suppose you think you're so good you don't need to practice."

"That is not true!" exclaimed Claud. "I may be good, but I'm not stuck-up."

"Are you calling me stuck-up?"

"*NO.*"

"Well, I'm going to take some runs. Maybe even a lesson."

"Okay."

"Okay."

"*Okay.*"

For the rest of the afternoon, Claudia and I skied the advanced trails under the watchful eyes of instructors. I hated to admit that Claud was better than I — but she was. Everyone knew that she was the best skier in our whole school, and I was second best.

Even so, I couldn't help yelling out to her as we shushed down a slope, "Our team is going to cream your team on Friday, Kishi!"

CHAPTER 13

Claudia

winsday afternon

I will never juge anything agian -- unless I'm juging totle strangers. The snow sclupture contest was awful all afternoon Kristy tryed to be really nice to me I know she whanted me to choose her teddy bear as the winning sclupture but it was just too cute for words. As juge I no better than to look for cute. I was looking for a well planed, well done not cute peice of work. The cheshur cat fit the bill. It was realistic and just a little bite mean looking. Ahsley is made at me too.

I would just love to see what Kristy wrote about the contest. I bet it's pretty different from what I wrote. I know she thinks I chose the Cheshire Cat because it won another contest for the Red Team, but that's just not true. I honestly thought it was the best sculpture, and Mr. Cheney, the co-judge, agreed with me.

I decided to ignore Kristy and Ashley and their angry, flashing eyes and take a free ski lesson. Kristy practically dared me to, anyway. I could have practiced on my own, but I thought, Hey, here I am at a ski resort with good instructors. I should take advantage of them. Maybe I can refine my technique.

So I went to the ski rental office and asked about lessons for advanced skiers. The woman there told me that a class was starting in just ten minutes.

"Great!" I exclaimed. "Thanks!"

I rode the ski lift to the top of the expert slope and there I found three kids from my team plus a few other people — and the most amazing-looking instructor in the history of skiing. His face was ruddy from being out-doors all day. His hair was blond and curly, his eyes were pale blue, and — best of all — he spoke with an accent.

"Hello," he greeted us. All us students were awestruck, especially the girls. "My name eez Guy." (He pronounced his name so that it rhymed with "ski.") "I am your eenstroctor. I trost zat you are very goode skiers."

"Oh, *very*," I couldn't help replying.

Guy smiled, showing a row of perfectly straight, sparkly white teeth. "Excellent. Zen let us get on wiss sings."

Sings? Oh, *things*.

"First, I woode like to see each of you take a ron down zee trail."

Where was Guy from? France? Switzerland?

I couldn't think about anything except his gorgeous face and his intriguing accent. If only he were a little younger. He looked about twenty-five. Well, maybe that didn't matter. I could fall in love with an older man . . . couldn't I? It happens all the time. I mean, to other people.

The members of my ski class were lining up to go down the expert trail. Guy spoke quietly to the first student and then she took off down the mountain. He watched her carefully. Then the next student went down, and then it was my turn.

"Zose are nice boots. Nice skis, too," said Guy approvingly, looking my equipment over. "Zose are not from zee lodge, are zey?"

"Oh, no," I replied. "They're mine. I go skiing all the time." (That wasn't *quite* true.) "I'm more comfortable with my own skis and stuff."

Guy nodded and smiled. "I onderstand. Now. Let me see whot you can do."

I drew in a deep breath and let it out slowly. I wanted to do my best for Guy.

So down I went. I concentrated very hard. I tried to remember everything I'd been taught. When I reached the bottom, I knew I'd performed well. I returned to Guy, feeling pretty pleased. But when I saw the expression on his face, my pleasure turned to joy.

"Marvelous!" he exclaimed. "Claudia, zat wozz wonderful!"

Claudia. He called me Claudia! I was pretty sure he'd been calling everyone else Miss or Mrs. or Mr.

"Thanks — thanks, Guy," I said breathlessly.

Guy smiled. And then . . . he put his *hand* on my *arm*. "Let me jost geeve you a few pointers. You can improve your speed by . . ."

I was listening to Guy. I really was. But I couldn't help noticing that not far from our group, another class was starting up. A young woman stood before a group of intent students. And one of those students was Kristy. She saw me at the same time I saw her.

Can you believe it? She actually stuck her tongue out at me. Right there in front of Guy and her instructor and all the students. Boy, what a sorehead. Just because the Blue Team had lost in ice-skating and snow sculpture. Of course, it did mean that if the Blue Team were going to win the Winter War, they had to win the remaining three events. And that was pretty unlikely. (By the way, in case you're wondering, if the Red Team won the next event — which meant we'd won the war —

the skiing competitions would be held on Friday anyway. They were too much fun to miss.)

"Claudia?" Guy was saying. He touched my arm again.

"Oh. Yes?" How could I concentrate if he was going to keep touching my arm?

"You need to change your pozeetion slightly. Like zees." Now Guy practically had his arms around me. I looked over at Kristy to see if she was watching us.

She was.

I wished I could have stuck my tongue out at her, but I am much too mature to do a thing like that when a handsome older man has his arms around me.

"Okay," I said to Guy. "I see what I'm supposed to do now."

"Goode. Now take anozzer ron down zee trail."

Anoz — ? Oh, another run down the trail.

"All right," I said.

I let myself fly. There is nothing in the world so wonderful as that feeling of motion and speed as you sail along over snow. Unfortunately, I noticed that at the same time I let loose, so did Kristy. She wasn't far away. And, darn her, she edged toward me so that soon we were skiing side by side down the mountain. I really hate having someone so close to me when I'm on skis.

I thought that over and changed my mind when I realized that Guy could have been skiing two inches from me and I would have been delighted. But Kristy was several feet away and that was too close.

"Move over!" I shouted at her. The wind was in my face but she heard me anyway.

"Making you nervous?" she yelled back.

"No! You're in my way!"

"I am not. And anyway, our team is going to cream your team on Friday, Kishi."

"No, you're not. Besides, it won't matter if you do because we're going to win the snowball fight tomorrow and then the war will be over."

Kristy shouted some sort of reply, but I put on a burst of speed and shot ahead, so I couldn't hear what she said. And I managed to stay ahead of her and even beat her back up the mountain again. Back to Guy. . . .

"Claudia! Again zat wozz magneefeecent. You are a chompion!"

A chompion? *Me?*

Guy took my hands in his (well, my fat mittens in his fat mittens) and said solemnly, "Next time, I want complete concentration.

133

Onderstand? Do not let yourself be dees-
tracted on zee trail. You weel be surprised at
how moch better you can do."

"Okay," I said. At least, I think I said it. I
was looking into Guy's eyes, which were
sparkly and bright. Then I looked at his lips
and couldn't help imagining myself kissing
them. I'm not sure whether any sound came
from my own lips.

Something must have, though, because Guy
said, "Very goode. Now go — and concentrate." He patted my shoulder.

Well, of course I went soaring down that
mountain. Kristy tried to psych me out again
by skiing practically on my heels, but all I
could think of was pleasing Guy. I was able
to ignore Kristy completely and beat her back
up the mountain again, where Guy put his
arms across my shoulders and called me his
star pupil.

I grinned from ear to ear. And then, unfortunately, I realized that after one more run
down the mountain I would have to go back
to the lodge. It was almost dinnertime, and I
should probably help with the Conway Cove
kids.

So I said a sad good-bye to Guy and got
ready for one last run.

"I weel see you tomorrow, no?" said Guy.

"Anozzer lesson for my star pupeel?"

No? *Yes!* Yes, of course he would see me. I would do anything Guy wanted. I would go over a ski jump and turn a somersault in the air if he thought I could do it.

I tried to appear suave and sophisticated, though, so all I said was, "Of course. Tomorrow." I wished I could speak whatever Guy's native language was.

I was about halfway down the mountain when a thought struck me, a guilty thought. *Will Yamakawa.* He was this guy I'd met at Camp Mohawk and we had *really* hit it off. He didn't go to my school, though. He didn't even live in my town, so we hadn't seen each other since camp ended. But we had written lots of letters and cards, and every now and then we spoke on the phone. Once, we had talked for an entire hour.

Was Will my boyfriend? I had thought I was in love with him when we were at camp. And I had to admit that I felt a funny thrill in my stomach every time I saw his return address on a letter. But that feeling was nothing compared to what I felt for Guy.

When I returned to the lodge, I couldn't help it: I raced up to our dorm, found Stacey, pulled her into a corner, and said (not very quietly), "My ski instructor has a crush on me. His name is Guy, he's adorable, and he talks with an accent!"

"Oh, wow!" cried Stacey.

"Oh, wow!" cried Dawn. Then she added, "Sorry. I couldn't help overhearing."

"That's okay," I replied.

By dinnertime, all the BSC members, plus a few other friends, knew about Guy and me.

I didn't mind. I was proud of it.

CHAPTER 14

Jessi

Wednesday afternoon
our team won the
snow-sculpture contest! I
am so excited. If the
Red Team wins the snow-
ball fight tomorrow, then
we've won the war. It's
too bad that Mal's and
my snow ballet slippers
didn't win, but I think
Claudia and Mr. Cheney
liked them a lot. They
stopped and looked at
them for a long time
and even whispered to
each other about them.
Oh, well.

After the contest was
over, I held auditions
for the talent show. It

is going to be so, so fun, and funny. Guess what— the teachers want to do a number of their own. Of course, I have to let them.

"Time's up!" called Kristy. "Everybody stop what you're doing. The judging of the snow sculpture contest is about to begin. Mr. Cheney and Claudia will be around to examine each sculpture. Please stand with your hands behind your backs."

"Oh, for pity's sake," muttered Mallory, and I giggled. She sounded exactly like her mother.

"Kristy loves rules. You know that," I said. One thing I've learned is that everybody, even the people you like best in the world, have faults, or do things that bug you. If you want to remain friends with those people, then you choose to overlook their faults. I overlook Kristy's bossiness and love of rules. After all, she let me into her club at a time when a lot of people in Stoneybrook didn't like our family. Kristy's attitude was, "Who cares? *I* like

Jessi, we *all* like Jessi, she's a good baby-sitter, so she stays." I have never forgotten that about Kristy.

Anyway, I'm completely off the subject.

So Mal and I were standing like fools with our hands behind our backs, waiting for Mr. Cheney and Claud to evaluate the mammoth pair of snow ballet slippers we'd patted into shape. You could see the ribbons winding up the ankles and everything.

Next to our shoes three kids had built a massive snow castle (not too original when you consider that people on beaches always build castles). On our other side was a snow model of the Wicked Witch of the West from *The Wizard of Oz*. Claud and Mr. Cheney walked from sculpture to sculpture, studying each one and whispering.

I watched them carefully. They stood for an awfully long time by one sculpture and when they moved away I saw that it was of the Cheshire Cat from *Alice in Wonderland* — and that the kids who made it had tinted it with food coloring!

"Is that *fair?*" I exclaimed to Mal.

"I guess so," she replied. "Kristy didn't say we could *only* use snow. In fact, she didn't mention any rules except the time limit. And standing here with our hands behind our backs."

"Darn. Why weren't we more creative? Well, at least the Cheshire Cat's on our team."

After Claudia and Mr. Cheney considered forever, the Cheshire Cat won. (Kristy looked like she wanted to kill Claudia.) When the winner was announced, I made another announcement, reminding kids about the auditions for the talent show, and then everyone who'd been sculpting on the lawn went off in different directions. Quite a few came to the grand ballroom to try out for the show.

Whew. Ever since I'd agreed to organize Talent Night a worry had been plaguing me: What if no one wanted to be in the production?

I should have known better. We are a bunch of show-offs. I had even brought my *Swan Lake* costume with me and planned to dance a solo number. I'd decided that was my personal right as talent-show coordinator. (I also wanted to ensure that there would be at least one number in the show.)

"Okay, everybody," I shouted to the twenty or thirty kids who were milling around the ballroom. I stood up on the stage so they could hear me better. "Those of you who have numbers rehearsed, stand on that side of the room," I said, pointing. "The rest of you stand on that side. I've got some ideas for you. Let me say in advance that the show is supposed to be forty-five minutes long, including the teachers' skit, which they tell me is seven minutes, so we've got thirty-eight minutes — more or less — to work with. If we run slightly overtime, no one will kill us. But I want you to understand that I will have to be a little picky. Not everyone can be in the show or it'll be too long. I'm sorry, but that's what Ms. Halliday told me, and she's the advisor for the talent show. Okay, let's begin with those of you who prepared skits or routines. I'll watch all of you and make my decision before you leave this afternoon."

Wow. As I stepped off the stage I felt pretty proud of myself. The kids were really listening to me. Not only was I a lowly sixth-grader, but I was the only black sixth-grader at SMS — and for that reason the kids either used to ignore me or jeer at me. But that was awhile ago, this was now. I was in charge, and everyone (even the eighth-graders) were listening.

"Okay, first number," I said. "Up on stage."

This seventh-grade girl, Davina, walked nervously onto the stage, sang some song called "Stop Pickin' on the President," and

141

then played a couple of choruses on a har-
monica with one hand while waving an Amer-
ican flag with the other.

I wrote her name on a pad of paper and put
a big NO next to it.

The second act was Alan Gray and a friend
of his, Rodge Somerset. They did a takeoff of
a vaudeville sketch. They were wearing top
hats and carrying canes, and they told corny
jokes like:

Alan: Hey, Rodge, did you get your hair
cut?

Rodge: Nope, I got 'em *all* cut!

Jessi

And, Alan: Did you hear about the fire down at the shoe factory?

Rodge: No, what happened?

Alan: A thousand soles were lost!

Their sketch was actually funny. I decided it was a possibility.

For the next hour, I watched act after act. A sixth-grade girl tap-danced to "Singin' in the Rain," wearing a raincoat and rain hat. Three seventh-grade boys did a tumbling act which was pretty good, and three seventh-grade girls dressed up as the old-time Andrews Sisters and lip-synched to "Don't Sit Under the Apple Tree." An eighth-grade boy who billed himself as "The Flooglemeister" juggled three bananas while playing a kazoo and balancing a ski boot on his head. Then four girls put on a skit that was a ghost story and both scary and funny. The last act I watched was this boy who could play all of "Doe, a Deer" with his armpit.

I studied my notes. Then I announced the acts that I'd chosen for the show. I could see a lot of disappointed faces, so I added, "If your act wasn't selected, come join the other group of kids. You can try out for something else."

I was glad I'd organized the tryouts this way. See, I knew there'd be some kids who were just dying to be in the show but really weren't that talented or didn't know what to do with themselves. I also knew that the teachers would be happy to see some nice normal acts in the show. So I had written a skit about Leicester Lodge with lots of parts in it, and I had also arranged a simple song-and-dance routine to a fifties song that I like a lot called "Chains of Love."

When I had selected kids for those numbers and rehearsed each number twice, I sent Mal (who had volunteered to be my helper) off to find Mary Anne and the kids from Conway Cove. She found them quickly — they'd been waiting eagerly for the ballroom to clear out so they could get on with their part in the show — and they raced over to me.

"I know what I want to do! I know what I want to do!" the kids were shouting. They were jumping up and down, except for Pinky, who was still supposed to be taking it easy on her foot.

"Okay, okay. One at a time," I said with a smile.

"Me first!" cried Joey. "Look at this. I can pretend I'm in a circus. See? First I'll pretend I'm a man on the flying trapeze. Then I'll be a bear on roller skates. Then I'll be a . . . *grrr* . . . lion tamer!" Joey proceeded to put on a one-man circus.

144

"My turn! My turn!" said Ginnie. "I can recite Shakespeare."

"*Shakespeare?!*" I couldn't help exclaiming.

"Yup. My big sister is in high school and she's in the drama club and she teaches me things all the time. Listen to this: 'A bee or not a bee. This is a question. If it's more noble to die, well, then I'll just have to die with my boots on.' "

I don't know much about Shakespeare, since we haven't studied any of his plays yet, but what Ginnie had said sounded . . . odd.

When Ginnie was done, Amber wanted to do a four-legged tap dance. She said she could put tap shoes on her feet *and* her hands and dance to "How Much Is That Doggie in the Window?" She also said that all four of her tap shoes were back in Conway Cove.

At this point I broke in and said, "Mary Anne, I thought you were going to help the kids write a *skit*. We don't have time for a million numbers — just one. What happened?"

Mary Anne shrugged. Her head had been in the clouds all week.

"Kids," I said. "I hate to disappoint you, but we have time for just one number. I was thinking you could put on a skit. Everyone could be in it."

"What kind of skit?" asked Pinky dubiously.

"Well . . ." I paused. The kids would probably think a fairy tale would be too babyish. But maybe — "How would you like to put on a skit about your school in Maine and your teachers? You know, *you* could be the teachers. You could be mean and order people around and complain about the way children behave in the cafeteria."

The kids' eyes lit up. A chance to get back at their teachers!

"Yeah!" cried fifteen voices.

The sixteenth voice said, "No way." That was Pinky. "We'll get in trouble. Miss Weber and Mr. Dougherty will see us!"

"Oh, they'll think it's funny," I said. "They'll understand."

"Will not."

"Will too. So that's settled. We'll parody Conway Cove Elementary."

The kids cheered, except for Pinky, who narrowed her eyes at me. I narrowed mine back. Pinky was just going to have to accept that black or not, I was in charge.

"She is so prejudiced," I said to Mal later.

But for once, Mal didn't agree with me. "I really don't think that's the problem this time," she told me.

But I knew better.

CHAPTER 15

Dawn

Thursday morning

I woke up in my bunk today feeling lower than low. It was awful knowing that Mary Anne was not in the top bunk, and furthermore, that she wasn't speaking to me.. (Mary Anne, are you really going to put all this stuff in your book for Logan? Try to tone it down a little, okay? It's embarrassing.)

The day was gray as usual (has the sun shone once since we arrived?) and tonight the storm was supposed to hit. The big storm. Why didn't they evacuate us? I guess they *thought we'd be safer if we stayed put than if we tried to travel home.*

I hate having someone mad at me.

"Rise and shine!" called Kristy cheerfully from her bed. "Time to get up."

I sat up and hit my head on the bottom of Pinky's bunk.

"Hey!" she cried.

Claudia crawled sleepily out of her top bunk, stepping on Stacey's hand on the way down.

"Ow!" exclaimed Stacey.

Oh. So it was going to be one of those mornings.

My friends and I got dressed silently, except for occasional strained, polite conversation. Mary Anne and I were barely speaking, I was mad at Kristy, and Kristy and Claudia seemed pretty testy, too. Only Mal and Jessi were acting normal. Even Stacey seemed a little funny — all daydreamy. Spacey Stacey.

Mary Anne and I headed for the bathroom (after the boys had finished dressing), and reached the door at the same time.

148

"After you," I said coldly.

"Oh, no. After *you*." Mary Anne held the door open for me.

"Thank you very much."

"YOU'RE *WELCOME!*"

"Would you guys tone it down?" hissed Claudia, who was behind us. "You're making the kids nervous. What's with you, anyway?"

"Nothing," said Mary Anne and I at the same time.

Claudia raised her eyebrows. "Really?"

"Oh, all right. You forced me to say it. She's a sappy jerk," I said, pointing to Mary Anne.

"*I* am? What about you?"

"SHHH!" Claud closed the door to the bathroom, calling over her shoulder, "We'll be out in a minute. The bathroom's off limits." Then she looked at us. "Well?"

"Well, nothing," I said.

"Yeah," agreed Mary Anne.

"Look, you two are best friends. Best friends do not call each other 'sappy jerks.' " She paused.

Neither Mary Anne nor I said anything.

Claud sighed. "Okay. I guess the fight isn't any of my business. But would you please try to act civil in front of the kids? They've been through a lot this week and they really look up to us."

"You're right," I agreed. "Okay."

"Yeah," said Mary Anne.

So breakfast that morning went something like this:

Me: Mary Anne, could I please have the butter?

Mary Anne: Certainly. And enjoy it.

Me: Thank you *ever* so much.

Mary Anne: You are *ever* so welcome.

Kristy looked at us as if our heads were on backwards. Nevertheless, she was all business that morning. Shortly before breakfast ended, she stood up to make her usual morning announcement:

"The snowball fight will be held this afternoon from two until three. Remember, you can build forts and shelters, lay in supplies of ammunition — which means *snow*balls only, no slushballs — and the object of the fight is for one team to capture the other team's red or blue tennis ball that the team captains will have at the beginning of the fight, and which, by the way, must be hidden in the snow or a fort, *not* on a person.

"Please use the morning for ski practice or another practice snowball fight if you intend to participate in the remaining events."

Kristy sat down, looking flushed, and Jessi immediately stood up.

"One more thing," she said. "We'll be rehearsing for Talent Night from ten to twelve in the grand ballroom this morning. Anyone in the show must be at rehearsal."

I felt like a real dud. I wasn't going to be in Jessi's show and I just couldn't bring myself to practice for the snowball fight or the ski competitions. Not after what had happened the day before. And that wasn't like me. I am not a quitter. I like to think I have a tough skin. After all, I survived my parents' messy marriage followed by their messy divorce, our move from California to Connecticut, my brother's move *back* to California, and the Trip-Man — that jerk of a boyfriend Mom went out with before she began seeing Mary Anne's father seriously.

When breakfast was over, I hurried out of the dining hall, leaving the BSC members and the Conway Cove kids behind. I just didn't feel like being with any of them. They all knew something was wrong and if they'd asked what it was, I was now so upset that I probably would have burst into tears and made a big scene.

Once I'd escaped from the dining room, though, I wasn't quite sure what to do with myself. I was about to head into the library to look for a book of ghost stories (my favorite

151

way to escape) when someone tapped my arm and said, "Hey, Dawn."

I turned around. It was Dori Wallingford, a girl I sometimes hang around with. "Hi," I said, trying not to look depressed.

"Hi," she replied. "Emily and I and a couple of other kids decided to play Monopoly all morning." (Dori is very cool, but as unathletic as Mary Anne. She doesn't take part in the Winter War.) "Want to play? It's so yucky outside — freezing cold and really windy. We're going to play at that table by the fireplace."

"Well . . . sure," I replied, thinking that it would be pretty hard to humiliate myself playing Monopoly. The only thing I could fall off of was my chair, and that was unlikely.

True. But I soon found that there were other ways in which to humiliate myself — like landing in jail on practically every turn and then taking forever to get out. And consistently landing on the two properties on which Dori had built hotels. It wasn't long before I was entirely out of money.

"Gosh, I've never seen anyone lose so *fast*," said Dori.

I know she didn't intend to be mean, but her words caused something to be unleashed from deep inside me. I had this feeling that I was going to cry, so since I was bankrupt anyway, I excused myself and made a run for the first-floor bathroom. I hoped fervently that it would be empty.

It wasn't. Pinky was there. And *she* was crying. She was just sitting on the windowsill, her face in her hands, weeping as if her heart would break. When I saw her, I forgot all about needing to cry myself.

"Pinky!" I exclaimed. "What's wrong? Did something happen? Are you sick? Did you hurt your foot again?" (I was amazed at how much I sounded like my mother.)

"No," replied Pinky, sniffling. She wouldn't

look at me, but she didn't seem angry, just sad.

"Are you lonely?" I asked.

Pinky shrugged.

"You can go out and play or skate or ski, you know. The doctor said it would be okay today."

"I know."

"Don't you want to?"

Pinky shrugged again.

I had an idea about what was wrong. Since I didn't want to embarrass Pinky, I said, "I'll tell you something. I feel a little like crying, too. And you know why?"

Pinky finally looked at me. "Why?"

"Because I'm homesick."

"Really? You are? I guess I am, too."

"Oh." I nodded.

"I've never been away from home before," said Pinky in a rush. "But I've always been — what's the word? You know — I'm not afraid of anything. I go skateboarding fast, and I help my dad with his fishing business. I can steer the boat and I bring in lobster traps, too. And I'm in Little League in Conway Cove. I can do anything. But as soon as I got here, away from home, I felt like a baby. And now everyone has *seen* me act like a baby and I have to face my friends in school on Monday."

Wow. Well, that certainly explained a few things. Pinky was trying to cover up her fears by being overly bold. Only she came off as bossy and bratty, as nasty and uncooperative. I'd seen the other kids ignore her or leave her out. And I knew she'd been giving Jessi a hard time. Funny what being away from home can do to you.

And then I thought — maybe that's my problem, too. Oh, I'd been away from home plenty of times before. (And where was home, anyway? California? Connecticut? Both places?) But I wasn't used to being away with my entire school — with all the kids I'd have to see day in and day out for the rest of the year. When I came to Leicester Lodge in seventh grade, I'd just moved here and hardly anyone knew me, so I didn't care what the other kids thought of me. And when I went to Camp Mohawk, I knew I wouldn't see most of those kids again, except maybe for two weeks the following summer. But now if I made a fool of myself at the lodge, I'd have to live with it for the rest of the year.

Suddenly I leaned over and gave Pinky a hug. "Thank you," I said.

"For what?" Pinky actually smiled.

"For teaching me a lesson." It was something I was going to have to think about and

155

deal with later — I wasn't as independent or as much of an individual as I'd thought. I would talk to Mom about it when I got home.

"Come on, Pinky," I said. "Let's go. I bet Curtis will make us some of his special hot chocolate."

CHAPTER 16

Mary Anne

Thursday

Dawn and I made up! I can't believe it! I was so happy!

What an afternoon this was, Logan. I wasn't in the snowball fight, but a couple of things happened. One of them -- you know what it was, of course -- was the best part of the whole trip for me.

We are very busy getting ready for the talent show tonight, but all anyone can talk about is the weather. No snow is falling yet. But it should start soon. Teensy Mosseman has upgraded her storm report from a ripsnorter to a dang-doozy. I'm a little nervous....

I was so surprised at lunchtime today. The last I'd seen of Dawn was at breakfast, when we'd had stupid, mean exchanges about butter and needing napkins and stuff. But when we met outside the dining hall at twelve-thirty, Dawn put her hand on my arm and said, "Mary Anne, let's talk, okay? Please?"

I almost said something really rude, but Dawn looked so earnest that I just replied, "Okay."

"We can go to our dorm," Dawn went on. "I don't think anyone will be up there."

She was right.

Dawn sat on her bunk and patted the blanket beside her, so I sat next to her. "Mary Anne," she began, "I want to say that I'm really sorry about the way I've been acting. I think I know what got into me. And I know what got into you, too — Logan. You miss him, and I should have been more understanding. But what you didn't know was how I was feeling."

"How you were feeling?" I asked.

Dawn nodded. Then she told me about her conversation with Pinky.

"Oh, Dawn," I said, and I could feel my eyes filling with tears. Why do I have to cry over every little thing? "I should have been

158

more sympathetic. I'm really sorry. All I could think about was Logan and me."

"Well, that's okay," Dawn replied, and *her* eyes filled with tears.

"No, it isn't." My tears spilled over.

"Yes, it is." Dawn's spilled over, too.

We were laughing and crying at the same time. Then I held my arms open and we hugged.

"Uh-oh," I said after a moment. "Lunch has started. We better get ourselves downstairs."

"Oh, we can be a few minutes late. There's something I have to do first."

"What?" I asked.

"This." Dawn ripped her blankets and sheets off of the bunk under Pinky's and moved them under mine again. "There. Everything's back to normal. *Now* we can go to lunch."

So we did.

I was *so* glad that Dawn and I weren't fighting anymore.

But soon lunch was over, the snowball fight had started (Dawn found the courage to join it, which made me very proud of her), and I found myself in the common room, alone with my book for Logan. I longed to talk to one of my friends, but Mal, Kristy, Dawn, and Clau-

159

dia were in the fight; Jessi was in the grand ballroom with Ms. Halliday, preparing for the show; and I didn't know where Stacey was. She'd been pretty scarce ever since Tuesday morning.

So I opened a notebook and started a letter to Logan, in Aruba:

My dearest, darling Logan,
How I miss you. How I pine for you. How I yearn and long for you.
My life is not the same without you. You are in my every thought during the day, and my every dream during the night.

I paused. Maybe I was going a little overboard. I didn't want Logan to think I wanted to marry him or something. So I turned to a blank page and started another letter:

Dear Logan,
I miss you. How is Aruba? Leicester Lodge is fine. Having a wonderful time. Wish you were here.

Well, that was pretty dumb. That was the kind of card you would send when you'd gone to some dinky tourist trap and were writing to someone you barely knew, like an eighty-five-year-old great-aunt who has blue hair and stuffs Kleenex up her sleeves.

I looked over my letters to Logan. I knew I wasn't even going to send them, so I just sat and thought. When I was finally able to drag my mind away from Logan, I mentally went over the skit that the Conway Cove kids were going to put on. I decided it would have to be changed. It was too . . . I don't know . . . juvenile. And it was kind of clichéd. It had been done a thousand times before. The kids should do something really original.

I put my pen in my mouth. Then I took it out and began scribbling ideas for a new sketch. It was all about a girl who was breaking up with her boyfriend. Kara, who was sophisticated for her age, and also one of the older girls, would be perfect for the female lead. She was sort of a feminist anyway, so she'd be apt to get riled up when she thought her boyfriend treated her unfairly. And Ian, who had strict ideas about what boys and girls can and can't do, would be great for Kara's chauvinist boyfriend.

I wrote and wrote and wrote. When I

thought the play was pretty polished, I ran into the grand ballroom with it.

"Jessi!" I called.

Jessi was gathering props with Ms. Halliday, but she ran over to me.

"Hi!" she said. "What's up?"

"I've rewritten the sketch for the little kids. I think it'll be much more appealing to the audience. What do you think?"

Jessi took the script from me and read it in silence. She pursed her lips. Then she put her hand over her mouth. I could see her dimples, though, which meant she was smiling. But when she removed her hand, she looked like our regular old Jessi.

"Um, Mary Anne," she began, "this skit is — is good. Honest, it is. But I'm not sure it's right for the kids. Besides, they love the idea of making fun of their teachers, and anyway, they've already learned the first skit. They don't have time to learn a new one. The talent show will be just a few hours from now."

"You're right. I didn't think of that," I replied, feeling a little foolish. "Sorry I interrupted you."

"Hey, no problem. I'm glad you're so interested in the show."

162

"Is there anything I can do to help you?" I asked.

Jessi looked thoughtful. "I guess not right now," she answered after a moment. "But I'll need you at rehearsal."

"Okay," I replied.

I wandered back out to the common room and sat down with my notebook. I looked over the information I'd gathered on the lodge and Hooksett Crossing. I actually had a fair amount. I'd be able to write the essay without any trouble as soon as I got home.

So I began yet another letter to Logan. I had gotten as far as, "Dear Logan, light of my life," when a man behind the check-in desk said loudly, "Is there a Mary Anne Spier here? A Mary Anne Spier?"

I stood up, startled. "I'm Mary Anne Spier," I told him.

"Oh, good. I tried your dorm and there was no answer, so I thought I'd page you. I'm glad you're here. I've got a long-distance phone call for you."

A long-distance call? For *me*? I was amazed. As far as I knew, no other kid from SMS had gotten a call here except for nerdy Alvin Hopper. His mother had phoned to make sure he was taking his allergy pills. No one could believe it. I hated to be placed in the same league as wheezy Alvin.

But then something occurred to me. A long-distance call could only be from one person — my father. And he wouldn't phone unless there was an emergency. Right away, I was sure something was wrong. My mind began racing:

Dad had had a heart attack and was in the hospital.

Dad had been in a car accident.

Our house had burned down.

Tigger had been hit by a car.

I wished Dawn were there to hold my hand while I took the call, but I knew I would have to be brave and handle the situation myself.

I took the phone gingerly from the desk clerk and faced into a corner so no one would see me when I started to cry.

"Hello, Dad?" I said.

"Mary Anne?" ventured the voice on the other end of the line. "This is Logan."

"LOGAN?!" I screeched. Then I remembered where I was and lowered my voice. "Logan! Where are you? I can't believe it's you!"

"Well, it is. And I'm down here in Aruba. How are you? I've been thinking about you day and night."

164

"Oh, me, too. I mean, *I've* been thinking about *you*. How's Aruba?"

"Fine, but I miss you."

"You do?"

"Of course. Don't you miss me?"

"Oh, *yes*. I can't tell you how much. So what are you doing? What's the weather like? Have you met any nice gi — any nice people?"

"A few. There's this family from Piscataway, New Jersey, in the room next to ours. They have a girl — "

"A *girl*?" I gasped.

" — exactly Hunter's age."

I sighed with relief. Hunter is Logan's little brother.

"What's going on at the lodge?" Logan continued. "I'm having fun here, but I kind of wish I were with you guys in Vermont."

"Oh, Logan, you won't believe what's happened this week." I told him about the two bus accidents and the children from Maine. I told him about my fight with Dawn, about Claudia and Kristy's ski war, and about the talent show. "Plus," I went on, "we're supposed to get a *huge* storm here tonight. We might even get snowed in."

"Well, don't get snowed in past Sunday. I'll die if I can't see you when I come home."

"You will?" I said in a small voice.

"Figuratively speaking."

"Oh, Logan. I love you."

"I love you, too, Mary Anne."

I hung up the phone, feeling like a new person.

CHAPTER 17

Mallory ♡

Thursday evening

The storm hit at exactly six-fifteen tonight, right in the middle of dinner. The snowball fight had ended in howling wind and freezing temperatures. (The Blue Team won, as you know, Mary Anne, so Kristy is overjoyed, certain that now her team will win the Winter War.) Anyway, in the middle of dinner, someone cried, "Hey, it's snowing!" and sure enough, it was. Tiny flakes were falling thickly and furiously. I don't want to be snowed in unless we can be evacuated tomorrow.

By the way, my journal project is not going too well.

Not going too well? My journal project was a failure, unless you consider learning from big mistakes to be a success. But I didn't want to admit that to Mary Anne or any of my friends. Two things had gone wrong: One, I'd been caught spying a couple of times. Two, hardly anything that I thought I'd observed had actually happened.

For starters, the cook (whose name I found out is Curtis) is probably not crazy. Anyway, he isn't trying to poison us all. If he were, somebody would be dead by now, but everyone's fine, all bodies are accounted for. I sneaked into the kitchen to try to find out what the stuff was I'd seen Curtis sprinkling into the food, but Curtis sneaked up on *me* and nearly scared me to death.

The powder was probably garlic or parmesan cheese. Sometimes people keep them in unlabeled jars.

Then, just this morning, I was tiptoeing around the lodge with my journal and I came across Stacey and this boy Pierre she's been spending so much time with. I passed by the doorway to the library and they were in there alone, sitting very close together on a couch. I thought that maybe if I stood outside and peeked at them through the crack in the door,

I could find out just what goes on when a boy and a girl kiss. (I've been *dying* to know.) But I hadn't been there long when Pierre said softly to Stacey, "Either I'm crazy or that door has eyes."

Stacey was off the couch and in the hall in a flash. She caught me red-handed!

"Mallory!" she exclaimed. "What are you doing?"

"Nothing," I replied, which is the best answer to give when you know you're doing something that someone will disapprove of.

"Are you sure?"

"Positive," I replied, trying to hide my journal. I escaped in a hurry.

The last thing that happened was the one that convinced me I knew nothing at all about observational skills. I didn't need to *hone* them, I needed to *acquire* them. Remember when I saw Ms. Halliday crying in the bathroom and decided it was because she was in love with the vice-principal (don't worry, he's not married or anything), but that he didn't love her back? Well, later I overheard her talking to Mary Anne and it turns out she's engaged to someone in Stoneybrook and she was just upset because she missed him.

Maybe, I decided, spying was not the best method for gathering information. Or if it was, I'd have to learn how to do it without reading all sorts of things into what I saw and letting my imagination run away with me. Like Jessi. She decided that Pinky's nasty behavior was a result of being prejudiced. But if Jessi had opened her eyes and looked beyond her own problems, she'd have seen that Pinky was having some trouble being away from home. And furthermore, that she was being upleasant to everyone, not just Jessi.

Anyway, back to Thursday evening. That night was a big one. Not only had the storm hit, but it was Talent Night and Jessi was in a frenzy. *Plus*, before the show began, all us SMS students were to gather in the common room, where a roaring fire was going, and where we were going to be served Curtis' famous hot chocolate. (I was glad I didn't need to worry about his poisoning us anymore.)

While we drank the hot chocolate, we were going to tell ghost stories! I was afraid that the Conway Cove kids, who were invited since they were going to be in the show later, would be too scared, but they insisted on coming.

"I know they're going to have bad dreams all night. I just know it," I told Jessi.

But Jessi was too busy worrying about the show to answer me.

At seven o'clock, we gathered in the common room. Now, that room is big, but I have to admit that seating the sixth-graders, seventh-graders, eighth-graders, and the Conway Cove kids, the SMS teachers, the Georges, and Curtis (who was pouring his hot chocolate into Styrofoam cups) was a bit crowded. We were jammed all over the floor, the couches, and the chairs. But I felt cozy and excited with the storm whistling and blowing outside.

When the hot chocolate had been served, Mr. Cheney stood up and said, "Attention, and welcome to the ghostly portion of Talent Night." (Everyone laughed.) "We'll be telling our scariest stories for the next hour, and then we'll move to the grand ballroom for the show. By the way, the teachers get to tell their stories first. That's one of the prerogatives of being a teacher." (Sometimes Mr. Cheney likes to impress us students with big words. In case you don't know what "prerogative" means — and I didn't — it's a special right or privilege.) "Anyone who wants to tell a story," Mr. Cheney went on, "just raise your hand and come stand before the fire so the others can see and hear you."

At that point the lights dimmed, and Mr. Cheney himself walked to the fireplace. The room grew quiet. All around me, kids leaned forward slightly.

"My story," Mr. Cheney began in a low, spooky voice, the firelight flickering behind him with an eerie glow, "takes place in a nice, normal neighborhood. It could be your neighborhood in Stoneybrook." (I shivered.) "On Silver Fox Lane lived a young woman. She wasn't married, but she had a good job and had just bought a house that she loved. However, she'd always been nervous about living alone, so she also bought a big guard dog, Butch, to protect her.

"One night, the woman came home and found the front door to her house ajar. Right away, she became scared. She knew someone had broken in.

" 'Butch!' she called. 'Butch?'

"She didn't hear a sound, so she flicked on the light in the entryway. She saw blood everywhere — but nothing seemed to be missing. She could see her TV and her tape deck in the living room.

"Now the woman was smart and knew she should get out of her house and call the police, so she did. When they arrived, they searched everywhere. The only unusual thing they found, apart from the blood, was Butch lying unconscious on the kitchen floor. The woman screamed. Then she rushed Butch to the vet, and the vet performed emergency surgery. And do you know what he found in Butch's stomach? . . . A man's finger. Butch had torn it off the intruder when he broke into the house, and had accidentally swallowed it."

All around me kids were gasping.

"Oh, *ew*," I said to Jessi. "That is so gross. Do you think it's true?"

Jessi looked at me wide-eyed. "It could be," she whispered. And boy was she surprised when, right then, Pinky scrambled into her lap for safety.

Mallory

We hardly had time to think about Pinky, though, because as soon as Mr. Cheney returned to his seat on the couch, Ms. Halliday stood up.

"My story," she began, "is about a man and a wife who were on their honeymoon. They were driving along a deserted road very late at night, listening to the radio. Suddenly an old Beatles song was interrupted by a newsflash. 'We have just learned,' said the announcer, 'that an insane murderer has escaped from the Towson County Jail. Please do not go out alone, and keep all your doors and windows locked. Thank you.'

"Well, the couple was scared to death. And wouldn't you know, just as the announcement was ending, one of their tires blew out, so the man left the woman alone in the car while he went looking for a gas station. He had been gone for about fifteen minutes when the woman started to hear a faint scratching sound, like this — *scritch-scratch, scritch-scratch* — on the roof of the car."

At that moment, every light in the lodge went out.

"Aughhh!" we screamed. Even the eighth-grade boys screamed.

Jessi tried to grab me, but Pinky was hugging her too tightly.

174

"He's here! He's here!" cried some kid. "It's the insane murderer!"

"No, it's the Leicester Lodge ghost!" exclaimed Curtis.

"Hey, hey, hey!" I recognized Mr. George's voice. "Hold your horses. The power's gone out, that's all. It happens nearly every time we have a big storm. Just sit tight and I'll turn on the emergency generator."

The room grew silent. I watched a flashlight bob away, the figure of Mr. George behind it.

"Shall I continue my story?" asked Ms. Halliday.

"NO!" we screeched.

A few more silent moments passed. They seemed like weeks. Then Pinky said in a whisper that was almost a sob, "We're going to get snowed in, aren't we? We're going to get stuck here. We'll never be able to go home, and the insane murderer will kill us all."

"Maybe they'll evacuate us tomorrow," Jessi said uncertainly to me.

Evacuate us tomorrow? Really? If that happened, there would be no all-school dance. I wouldn't have to go! Despite the storm and the power failure, I began to feel a little better. I prayed for a gigantic storm and an evacuation.

But Mr. George spoiled it all. The lights

came back on, and a few minutes later he reappeared saying, "Good news. I just heard a weather report. Now they're saying that the storm is supposed to pass to the east of us. The worst is probably over. When you wake up tomorrow, you'll find sunshine and about four inches of fresh snow for your ski competitions."

DARN.

No blizzard and the dance would be held after all. And there didn't even seem to be any sign of the ghost Mary Anne had told about. I guessed the "ghost" was just another ghost story.

Ms. Halliday finished her story. "So, anyway," she said, "the woman waited all night for her husband to return. He never did. But the woman heard the scratching noises until the next morning, when a police car pulled up alongside her.

" 'Stay in the car, lady!' shouted a police officer.

"The woman followed his instructions. There was a huge scuffle, and a man was pulled off the roof of her car, handcuffed, and led to the squad car. It was the insane murderer! He had killed her husband, and was after the woman. All night he had lain on the roof of her car where she couldn't see him, and had been scratching through it with his *fingernails*. Another eighth of an inch and he would have killed the woman, too!"

I nearly fainted. Then two more teachers told us tales that scared us to death. After that, kids started telling stories. We heard about ghostly hitchhikers, about campers who were the prey of escaped convicts, about some more honeymoon couples, and we heard one particularly scary story that Stacey's friend Pierre told, called "Three-Fingered Willie."

But I only half heard them. I couldn't stop thinking about the dance the next night. I knew I was going to make a fool of myself.

CHAPTER 18

Jessi

Thursday night

Hi, Mary Anne. Well,
you were there. You
were at the talent
show. So you know
what went on. Anyway,
this is mean, but
I just couldn't help
laughing (to myself) when
Dimples got mixed up
during her number. You
have to admit it was
funny. I also couldn't
help feeling very proud
after my own number.

What you don't know
about is what happened
after the show. It
happened between Pinky
and me, and part

of it was really nice, but the rest of it sure gave me something to think about. I'll have to talk to Mama and Daddy when I get home. Becca, too. I think we should call a family conference. I know I need one.

Oh, wow. Was I ever nervous before the show began! I had never been in charge of something as big as Talent Night. And I was going to be *in* the show, too. I thought that was fair. Besides, there were a few kids that I needed to show off in front of. But I had to be sure and do a good job.

When the scary stories were over and the hot chocolate was finished, us SMS students moved into the grand ballroom. It had been set up like a theater. There was the stage with a curtain at one end of the room, and now row after row of folding chairs had been set up so that everyone would have a place to sit down.

While the audience settled into the chairs, I ran backstage with the kids who were going

179

to be performing. I quickly counted heads. Everyone was present.

"Okay," I said, "I think you know the order in which you're supposed to go on stage, but in case you forget, I've posted the listing in the wings. Remember, the teachers go first, the Conway Cove kids go last, and when the show is over, we all run on stage in two lines, holding hands, for the curtain call.

"Now all the props are over there," (I pointed to a sturdy folding table) "and Callie is in charge of the music. If you need music for your number, just hand her your tape before you go onstage and she'll put it in the tape deck. Any questions?"

There weren't, so I tapped Terry Morgan on the arm and said, "You're on, Mr. Announcer."

As coordinator of the show, I guess *I* could have been the announcer, but when Terry's plan to dress up like Father Goose and recite nursery rhymes in Italian wasn't accepted by me as an act for the show, he begged to do something — *any*thing. So I told him he could be the announcer. (Besides, I would have felt funny announcing myself later on.)

When I felt that the kids were ready to begin the show, I signaled Ms. Halliday, who signaled someone else, and the lights in the grand ballroom were dimmed, except for two bright ones on the stage.

I nodded to Terry, he nodded back, and then he stepped confidently onto the stage. "Good evening, ladies and germs," he began. (I had told him he could say that.) "Well, I just flew in from Stoneybrook and, boy, are my arms tired." (The audience groaned, but they were laughing, too.) "Anyway, welcome to Talent Night. We in the show have enjoyed preparing these numbers for you, and we hope you will enjoy seeing them. And now, without further adieu," (I had *not* told Terry he could say that), "may I present the SMSTs."

Terry walked offstage in one direction while the SMS teachers walked on from the opposite direction. There were eight of them, and they were all wearing red turtlenecks and blue jeans, and carrying microphones.

One teacher stepped forward and said, "Welcome to the Do-wop Stop." Then he stepped back in line. For the next seven or so minutes those teachers sang a medley of fifties hits. That in itself was pretty good because it turned out that these, like, math and social studies teachers could actually harmonize. But the fun part was that they'd changed the words of the songs, so they were singing about things like kids cutting classes, the noise in

Jessi

the cafeteria, the bus ride to Leicester Lodge, and even the Winter War. When they were done, they somehow seemed like real people to me, instead of just teachers. I guess they sounded like that to the rest of the kids, too, because they got a huge round of applause.

The next act was Dimples Howard (that was her stage name, of course), doing her tap number to "Singin' in the Rain." Terry introduced her as the Titan of Tap, but I don't think anyone knew what he meant.

"Wait till I reach the middle of the stage before you hit the Play button," Dimples told Callie as she handed her the cassette.

"Okay," said Callie.

Then Dimples, who was already wearing her raincoat, tied on a rain bonnet and stooped down to buckle one of her shoes. But the buckle broke and it took her so long to fix it that the audience got restless and Callie started the tape, just so people would have something to listen to. By the time Dimples ran onstage, the audience was listening to the end of the second verse of the song and Dimples couldn't find her place.

"Start it over!" she hissed to Callie, but Callie got flustered and fast-forwarded to some later spot in the song, so Dimples just sort of improvised until the song was over. When that happened, Dimples stayed onstage and demonstrated the single, double, and triple time steps as well as the Manhattan time step, so at least she felt she had shown what she was capable of doing.

The next act was a personal favorite of mine, partly because it involved no music. Bobby Henson, who had wanted to play "Doe, a Deer" with his armpit, which I wouldn't let him do, then decided to dress up as Lucille Ball and imitate her rehearsing this commercial for a product called Vitameatavegamin, which he assured me happened during an *I Love Lucy* show entitled "Lucy Does a TV Commercial."

"Hello, friends," Bobby began. (He was wearing a polka-dotted dress, and a ladies' hat and gloves, which was pretty funny by itself, so already kids were laughing.) "Are you tired, run-down, listless? Are you unpopular? Do you poop out at parties?"

Bobby had memorized the entire commercial — including the way Lucy started goofing it up. When he said, "Are you unpoopular? Do you pop out at parties?" I saw one kid in the audience laugh so hard that he began coughing and had to leave the grand ballroom for a drink of water.

The show continued. The Flooglemeister was a big hit, despite the fact that Terry introduced him as the Frugalmaster. The girls who imitated the Andrews Sisters were a hit, too. Then came the funny ghost story, the skit about Leicester Lodge, the "Chains of Love" number, and finally . . . my dance routine. After so much hilarity, I hoped the kids were ready for me because *Swan Lake* was serious, not funny.

The kids *were* ready. Even so, I was nervous, but I've danced in front of big audiences before, and I know how to tune out the people and pay attention only to the music and the movements of my body. So I turned and pirouetted in a world of my own, not returning to the real world until the music was over.

When I stopped dancing, there was a moment of silence. Then the kids and teachers, even the ones backstage, began clapping loudly. A few kids even whistled! I felt as if I had *finally, really* been accepted at Stoneybrook Middle School, which was why I grinned until my face nearly fell off.

The last act of the evening was the skit performed by the Conway Cove kids. They were looking a little tired from the excitement of the evening — the snowstorm, the power failure, the ghost stories, and the talent show — but they pulled themselves together nicely. When I gave them the cue, they ran out on the stage, introduced the characters they would be playing, and launched right into the skit. Not one of them forgot a line, and they spoke clearly and confidently, even Pinky, and thank goodness, because she had one of the funniest parts. She played a teacher named Miss Wyndham, who I gathered had been at their school for decades, and whose claim to fame was that she'd once gotten a grape stuck up her nose. Personally, I thought it was one of those stories that had never happened but was destined to circulate the school each year for as long as Miss Wyndham continued to teach.

At any rate, Pinky got tons of laughs.

So I was quite surprised to find her crying in the first-floor bathroom after the show. I'd headed in there to be by myself for a few minutes before tackling the job of helping my friends put the little kids to bed. I just needed some of what Mama calls "down time."

But there was Pinky sobbing over one of the sinks.

"Pinky! What's the matter?" I exclaimed. "Why are you crying? Your skit went perfectly. Everyone loved it. They especially loved you."

Pinky shook her head. "It's not that."

"It isn't? What's wrong?"

Pinky paused. Finally she said, "Just homesick, I guess." Then she added, "I know I was really mean to you this week, Jessi. I'm sorry."

I was so surprised that I didn't know what to say. Pinky must have thought I was angry, because she rushed on, "I've been mean to everyone, and I know it. I'm *really* sorry." She looked pleadingly at me.

"Oh, Pinky," I said. "That's okay. I mean, I did think you didn't like me, but I'm not angry. Not anymore."

Pinky began talking to me again, but I had a little trouble paying attention to her. I was remembering something that Mallory had said

to me, something about Pinky's not being prejudiced. And I was remembering Pinky bossing
the other kids around and the kids then ex-
cluding her from things.

Why was it that I had overlooked all that
and focused on what Pinky had said and done
only to me (like ordering me to get her a
drink)? Was it because of the bad experiences
I'd had in Stoneybrook with our neighbors?
Probably. But did that mean *I* was prejudiced
in some way now? I hoped not. But I knew I
would need to have a long talk with my parents when I returned from Leicester Lodge.

"Come on, Pinky," I said, holding my hand
out to her. "It's late. We should go to bed."

Pinky sighed softly. "Okay," she replied.

Hand in hand, we went upstairs to our
dorm.

CHAPTER 19

Claudia

Firday morning

Waht a bust. Mr. Goerge said the snowstrom would pass us bye and he was wright. Well it didn't excatly pass us by but we only got three inchis Im not complaning though. This is prefect for the ski compertitons which are downhill this monring and x - county this afternon. I'am pretty sure the red Team will wine!

Guess waht. The sun is shinning for the frist time today. Its a good thing I broght along my new ski gogles. They will be handy. More improtant ~~Die~~ Guy (Stacey helped me ~~speel~~ that) will be impresed I think.

The ski competitions. I'd been waiting for them all week. For me, they would be the highlight of the trip. They always are, especially downhill. And this time, Guy would be there to cheer me along. He had promised so on Thursday after giving me a private lesson. Note that I said *private*. How that happened was that on Thursday morning after I took a class with him I said, "Will you be teaching another class late this afternoon? The ski competitions are tomorrow and I could use some extra help."

What do you think Guy said? He said, "No, I do not have a class scheduled, bot for you I weel make an exception. How about a priveet lesson at sree-sirty?"

Sree-sirty? Oh, three-thirty.

"*Sure*," I replied.

So I had a private lesson with Guy. He was very helpful. But I have to say that I was having just a little trouble concentrating. At one point he positioned my body for the perfect ski stance. As soon as his mittens touched my parka, my mind went into orbit. It was flying around in outer space. All I could think of was Guy and me sitting in a darkened restaurant together. The maitre d' has given us a quiet, intimate table in the back with a candle in a glass holder in the middle of the table. By the flickering light, Guy takes my hand in his and says —

"Zat eez very goode. You are ready for your ron now."

No, no. That wasn't what he said in the daydream. That was what he said during the lesson.

I let myself fly. Down the mountain I went. And off into outer space went my mind again. This time, Guy and I are walking along a beach at sunset. In that lighting, the sand looks pink. To our right are palm trees with fat coconuts hanging from them. To our left is the ocean reflecting the setting sun. Guy and I are holding hands. We're laughing. We're —

Coming to the bottom of the mountain! I put on the brakes, but I knew the end of my run had been sloppy. Guy confirmed that when I got off the ski lift.

"If you want to be zee best tomorrow," he said, "you most not let your mind wander. Do you onderstand? You deed well, bot you can do moch better."

I nodded and took another run, this time allowing myself only a brief fantasy about sitting in a boat on a canal in Venice with Guy before dragging my mind back to skiing. I was later rewarded with an ear-to-ear grin from

Guy and a pat on the back. Or was it a small hug? I couldn't be sure.

Anyway, by Friday morning I knew I was ready for the downhill ski competition. It would be my best event, and I was pretty sure I could win it for my team. This is how the competition would work: The members of each team had been assigned to a beginner group, an intermediate group, or an expert group. (That was so beginners could be in the event without having to compete against experts. By the way, Kristy and I were in the expert groups on our teams, Dawn was in an intermediate group, and Stacey asked to be in a beginner group, although I think she could have competed with the intermediates.)

Each kid in each group, starting with the advanced skiers, would take a run downhill. They would be judged on both speed and performance by the head ski instructor at the lodge. The winning beginner would earn five points for his or her team, the winning intermediate seven points, and the winning advanced skier nine points. Therefore it was possible for one team to cream the other by winning all three categories, or for a race to be as close as one team earning nine points and the other twelve.

At breakfast on Friday, Kristy was impossible. "We're going to beat the pants off you guys," she said to me. "And then we'll beat you in cross-country so we'll have *won* the *war!*" She looked jubilant at the very thought.

"Big deal," I replied. "So you'll each get a piece of pizza. We've got frozen pizza at our house all the time. I can have it whenever I want."

"You know that's not what I mean," said Kristy.

"Yeah, all you think about is winning," I told her sarcastically.

"That's right." Kristy stuffed a piece of toast in her mouth. "Ishm *mat* the pot?"

"What?" I said.

Kristy swallowed. "Isn't *that* the point?"

Before the discussion could get any testier, Mal changed the subject. She turned to Pinky and the other little kids. "Who wants to go ice-skating this morning?" she asked.

"Me! I do!" cried most of them — including Pinky.

"You better start getting them dressed as *soon* as breakfast is over," Stacey whispered to Mal. "It could take hours to get them ready."

Not much later, the downhill skiing competition was about to begin. The advanced skiers had gathered at the top of the nearest mountain, the intermediates were further down, and the beginners were at the head of one of the baby trails. A big crowd of people was waiting at the bottom of the mountain. This Winter War event got more attention than any other, so we had a pretty good audience.

The most important member of the audience for me, however, was . . . Guy, of course. And *he* wasn't just milling around with the crowd below. *He* was standing at the top, still giving me pointers and an occasional pat on the back. (Hug?)

The advanced skiers were to take their runs first, and everyone knew that the real competition would be between Kristy and me, since each of us was the best skier on our respective teams.

The event began. The lodge's head ski instructor, Ms. Olsen, tossed a coin. My team had called heads — and we won the toss. Rick chose Lindsay McManus to lead, and off she went. She was good, and reached the bottom with a fast time. The next skier was Miranda Elliot from Kristy's team. She was even better and faster.

One after another the advanced skiers whipped down the slope. Finally, only Kristy and I were left. Kristy poised herself at the top of the run. I could almost see her gathering her concentration and shutting out everything but the slope and her skis.

Kristy earned the fastest time yet. When she heard the news she let out a yell. "All *right!* This event is in the bag for the Blue Team!"

I'll admit it. She was psyching me out. But just before I poised myself for my run, Guy touched my arm and whispered in my ear, *"Concentrate."*

I concentrated.

I also beat Kristy. I had earned nine points for our team! "You're wrong, Thomas!" I cried. "This event is in the bag for the *Red* Team!"

But as it turned out, I was wrong. I couldn't believe it. The Blue Team won in both the intermediate and the beginning competitions. They beat us twelve to nine.

"We're tied! We're tied!" Kristy shouted. "And the Blue Team is going to beat the Red Team in cross-country."

"How?" asked Rick. "Hardly anyone entered the event on your team. We've got all the good cross-country skiers."

"Do not," replied Kristy, which is a surefire way of letting people know that suddenly you're not so sure of yourself.

I looked at my watch. Lunchtime — and I was starved. The SMS kids made their way into the dining hall to fuel up before the last event of the Winter War. Although we had lost in downhill skiing, I felt like I was walking on air.

"Guy really likes me," I told the BSC members as we ate our lunch.

"But he's too old for you," said Mary Anne.

"Age doesn't matter," I replied, trying to sound as wise as my grandmother Mimi would have sounded if she'd still been alive.

"How can you be sure he really likes you?" asked Jessi.

195

"Oh, just by the way he looks at me. By the way he gives me encouragement, pats me on the back, wants to spend time with — "

I stopped talking. My eyeballs almost shot out of their sockets. I had looked away from Jessi and seen Guy approaching me. He was carrying a baby in one arm, a little girl was holding his free hand, and a beautiful woman was with him.

"Hello," said Guy. "Claudia, I wanted you to meet my family. Zees baby here eez Jean, zees leetle won eez my daughter, Marie, and zees eez my wife, Domitille. Domi, zees eez Claudia, zee wonderful skier I woz telling you about."

I don't know how I got through that conversation, but I did. I even managed to smile. When Guy and his family left, our table was silent. No one said a word, not even Kristy. In fact, she put her arm around me for a moment.

I tried to tell myself, It would never have worked out anyway. He really *is* too old. And then I thought, Thank goodness for Will. I've still got Will.

But my feelings had been wounded.

CHAPTER 20

Kristy

Friday afternoon

The cross-country skiing event was held this afternoon, Mary Anne. You didn't see it since the Conway Cove kids wanted to go traying on the lawn in front of the lodge and you agreed to watch them after Mrs. George gave the kids her permission. So you weren't around for what happened during the final event of the Winter War, although I'm sure you heard about it. It all began when I got carried away with myself at lunchtime....

I wish I'd had a camera with me in the dining hall so I could have captured the look on Claud's face when Guy walked over to her with his wife and kids. No, scratch that. I don't wish that at all. It would have been mean. Claud's feelings were *really* hurt. I think I'll remember the look on her face even without a camera.

And although I honestly did feel bad for Claudia, I guess I'm slightly mean (maybe everyone is, I don't know), because some teeny-tiny part of me couldn't help thinking, "If Claud is upset, maybe she won't do well in cross-country skiing this afternoon and her team will lose." Isn't that awful? But that's how I felt. I just wanted to win so *badly*. And the Blue Team was so *close*.

That was only the beginning of how I went win-crazy that afternoon, though. Next, I waited until Claudia had composed herself, and kids were starting to finish their lunches, before I tapped on my glass to make an announcement.

"Attention, Blue Team members!" I said. "Attention, please! As you know, this afternoon is our last chance to beat the Red Team. As you may *not* know, we don't have nearly enough good cross-country skiers signed up for this event. Come on, you guys! It's not too late to join the team. How many of you out there are willing to join so we can win the war?"

I thought I sounded like a coach giving his team a good pep talk, but instead of enthusiastic shouts, I just heard some murmurs and saw a couple of heads nod.

Cross-country skiing is not the most popular event to enter.

Oh, well. Desperate times call for desperate measures.

So first I asked Dawn to participate in the event. I received a flat-out no. She'd gotten through the snowball fight and downhill skiing (doing well, by the way), but wasn't about to risk trying a new sport. So I began walking from table to table. At each one I personally asked the Blue Team members to join the final event of the war.

"Anyone can cross-country ski," I said to Shawn Benedict. "Have you even been on regular skis?"

Shawn shook her head.

"Oh. Well, that doesn't matter," I went on. "If you can walk, you can cross-country ski. So join up, okay? We *really need* you."

"All right," said Shawn uncertainly. "If you promise it's that easy."

"I promise," I told her. I looked at Jay Marsden, who was sitting across from Shawn. "What about you? If you can walk, you — "

"I know, I know. If I can walk, I can ski," he said.

"So?"

"Gee, I don't know, Kristy."

"Come *on*. For our team. For the war. Where's your spirit?"

Jay looked embarrassed. "All right. I'll join."

"Great!"

I approached another table, but the kids there must have overheard my conversations with Shawn and Jay because before I could even open my mouth, three of them said, "We can't walk yet!"

"Spoilsports," I muttered as I headed for the next table. There I talked two more kids into entering the event. By the time lunch was over, the Blue Team had gained thirteen new contestants in cross-country skiing. Now we had twenty-eight contestants and Rick's team had twenty.

Since there was a full hour before the competition was to begin, I took all the novice skiers to the rental shop, helped get them fitted with cross-country skis, and gave them a fast lesson. I'm not much of a cross-country skier myself, but I figured I knew more than they did. Besides, all they'd be required to do in the event was ski a short trail.

This is how the competition would work: Groups of four kids — two from my team, two from Rick's — would ski similar-length trails at the same time. The kid who crossed the finish line first would score a point for his or her team. Since Rick's team now had fewer members than mine, some of his skiers would go twice. Rick would pick the best ones, of course . . . if they weren't too tired. I had a hunch that sheer numbers would make up for talent.

Our practice hour was, well, let's just say it was not ideal. Shawn couldn't stay up on her skis. I have never seen one person fall down so often in such a short period of time. She'd be up on her feet, then BOOM! in the snow, up on her feet, then BOOM! in the snow.

"Kristy," she said at last, "in case you care, I am not enjoying myself."

"Just try *one more time*," I begged her.

Shawn struggled to her feet. Her face was beet-red. But at least she stayed up. She seemed to be getting the hang of things.

Before I knew it, the hour was up and it was time for the competition to begin.

"Kristy," Jay said to me nervously, "I can stay on my feet all right, but I sure can't go very fast. I have a bad feeling about this."

"Don't worry," I told him. "No one's much good at this event. Honest."

I was half right. No one on *my* team seemed to be much good. At least not in the beginning. I hoped, though, that was because I was sending my most inexperienced team members out first, so they could get things over with and we would catch up later.

We lost race after race.

The lodge's cross-country ski instructor would stand by the line of kids who were competing in each round, shout, "Take your marks, get set, GO!" and *my* team members would barely get themselves moving while the other two kids would be halfway to the finish line.

I put Shawn in the first race so she could quit looking so uncomfortable. Suddenly, she seemed to be back in our practice session. The instructor shouted, "GO!" and immediately Shawn was sitting on her bottom. I felt pretty bad for her, especially when a few kids around us started snickering. Poor Shawn didn't even try to catch up with the others. She just removed her skis and watched Rick's team win the race.

I put Jay in the fourth round. He actually skied about three quarters of the way to the finish before he fell. But when he landed we all heard the *snap* and his agonized cry.

"Oh!" he shouted. "Help! I think I broke something."

In the blink of an eye, two teachers and the lodge doctor raced to Jay. The doctor and the other Blue Team member in the race (who was coming in last, of course) collided, but neither of *them* was hurt.

Jay wasn't so lucky, though.

"Don't move him," the doctor told the teachers. Then he said to the kids who were crowding around, "Stand back. Let him have some air." And he sent Mr. Cheney to call for the paramedics while he and Mr. George eased Jay onto a stretcher and moved him to the lodge.

Jay had broken his ankle. No one could really concentrate on the race after that. Rick's team halfheartedly beat mine.

The Blue Team had lost the event and the entire Winter War.

I couldn't believe it.

"This didn't happen," I said to Stacey when it was all over and we were walking back to the lodge. "We didn't lose."

"I'm a little more concerned about Jay than the war," Stacey replied crisply.

"But you barely know Jay," I pointed out.

Stacey gave me a Look.

The truth is, I was worried about Jay myself. I just didn't want to admit it. I knew the accident was my fault. I was responsible for it. If I hadn't pushed Jay so hard he would never have entered the cross-country ski event. But I had pushed, and Jay had entered, and he had fallen and broken his ankle. I guessed that everyone blamed me for it.

All of a sudden I knew I was going to do something I don't do very often — cry. I quickened my pace, pulled ahead of Stacey, and rushed into the lodge.

"Hey, where are you going?" Stacey called after me.

I couldn't answer her. I just kept going, moving faster and faster toward our room, all the time thinking what a horrible person I was.

By the time I reached our room, a huge lump had formed in my throat, and my eyes were brimming with tears. I sincerely wished that no one would be in the dorm.

I did not get my wish.

Mary Anne was helping two of the little kids remove mittens and boots and plastic bags. Wet clothing was draped everywhere — over chairs and beds and on the windowsills.

Luckily, Mary Anne took one look at me and saw that I was in trouble. She whisked Joey and Ian out of the room, sat me on a lower bunk, and said, "I guess we lost the war, didn't we?"

I nodded numbly. "But that's not the worst part," I managed to say. In between a lot of gulping and hiccupping, I told her about Jay Marsden.

"Well, that is pretty bad," Mary Anne said slowly, "but you know, you didn't *force* Jay to compete. He could have said no. He just *let* you push him into it."

"I do push people around, don't I?"

Mary Anne paused. At last she replied,

"Well, you're a lot better about it than you used to be."

"Sometimes I just don't understand myself," I told her. "Usually I'm totally competitive — but there are times when I can force myself not to be. Like with the Krushers." (The Krushers are a team of little kids that I coach in softball.) "I hardly ever push them around, even when we have a game coming up. I tell them that the point of a game is just to have fun. That should have been the point of the Winter War, Mary Anne. Maybe . . . maybe I get more competitive when I'm participating myself."

"Maybe," agreed Mary Anne. Then she gave me a hug.

"The kids all hate me," I told her with a sob.

"I doubt that," said Mary Anne.

As it turned out, she was right.

CHAPTER 21

Mallory ♡

Friday evening

I'm sorry, but to be perfectly honest, I
have to tell you that for a few brief, crazy
moments, I hoped that because of Jay's
accident, the all-school dance would be
called off for some reason. You know, like
in sympathy —— Jay couldn't dance, so we
wouldn't, either. Not only did that not happen
(darn the luck), but Jay was back at the lodge
and in fine shape by dinnertime. The break
had turned out not to be serious. Just two
small bones were fractured, but I guess
you already know that, Mary Anne. Anyway,
although I was glad to see Jay, I knew
that I was going to start some major
worrying. And I did....

I hoped for *anything* that would cancel the dance. I hoped the grand ballroom would burn down. I hoped the whole lodge would burn down. I hoped we'd all develop malaria.

"Jessi, Jessi, I'm going crazy," I said hysterically.

It was after dinner on Friday, and the stupid old all-school dance was supposed to start in less than an hour. Why hadn't the lodge burned down yet? I wondered. I'd wished hard enough for it.

"What's the matter?" asked Jessi.

"What's the matter? What's the *matter*? The dance is what's the matter."

Jessi looked at me blankly. I hadn't told her or anyone else my fears about the dance.

"It's — it's — I — I don't — I can't — "

"Mal, for heaven's sake, calm down. You're scaring the children," said Jessi.

The members of the BSC were returning to our dorm to get ready for the dance, and the Conway Cove kids were trickling in behind us.

I drew in a deep breath. Then I let it out slowly. "The dance. I've never been to one. I don't know how to dance. I didn't bring any good clothes with me. I'm going to make a fool of myself. Why can't it be Saturday already? Then we'd be home. The dance would be over. Well, I don't *really* want to leave Hooksett Crossing. This week has been fun. But — "

"Mallory," Jessi interrupted, "I've never been to a dance, either, but I'm looking forward to this one."

"That's because you can dance."

Jessi made a face. "I'm a *ballerina*. I can assure you that no one will be doing ballet steps tonight. However, if you would relax a little, you could dance just fine. Anybody can. Here." Jessi turned to Claud, who was looking into a mirror, carefully applying mascara to her eyelashes. "Claud, where's your tape player? Can I borrow it for a sec?" she asked.

"Sure," replied Claud. She handed it to Jessi, who looked through Claudia's tape collection, selected a tape, and slipped it into the player.

When the music came on, Jessi said, "Okay, watch me and then imitate what I'm doing."

Jessi began moving around, snapping her fingers.

I tried to imitate her, I really did, but Jessi stepped forward, put her hands on my shoulders, and said sternly, "*Relax*. You look like you're being carried off to jail. This is just a dance."

I tried again . . . and again. At last Jessi said, "Much better! See? That wasn't so hard, was it?"

"No," I admitted. But then I added, "I didn't bring a dress. I don't have anything to wear."

"Mallory, neither does anyone else. None of us knew about this dance until two days ago. They've never had an all-school dance here before."

I was about to say, "Then how come Claudia has mascara with her?" when I remembered that she wears it almost every day. "Oh, yeah," was all I said.

"So are you ready to get dressed?" asked Jessi. "Wear your red-and-white sweater with your jeans. That's a nice outfit."

"All right," I agreed.

The rest of my friends were trying to get ready, too, but it wasn't easy. Not with sixteen children hanging around. Most of them were watching us. The others were dancing to the music, which was still playing on Claud's tape deck. They were copying what they'd seen Jessi show me — and they weren't bad!

That was what gave me the idea. I suddenly thought, I bet the little kids would enjoy the dance. Then something else occurred to me. I ran over to Kristy (since she *is* the president of the Baby-sitters Club) and I said, "Hey, Kristy, what are the little kids going to do while everyone else is at the dance? We can't leave them alone."

"Wow, I can't believe I didn't think of that," said Kristy, although I could believe it. She'd been totally distracted ever since Jay broke his ankle.

"I guess Miss Weber or Mr. Dougherty will take care of them."

"I — I think the kids would rather go to the dance," I ventured.

"You do? But — "

"I'd be happy to watch them," I rushed on.

From nearby, Jessi frowned at me. She knew exactly what I was doing. If I had to watch the kids, then it wouldn't matter if no one asked me to dance. I could just tell myself it was because I looked too busy. Besides, the kids would probably have the time of their lives. They could drink punch and eat cookies. Everyone at the lodge thinks they're adorable anyway.

Of course, Kristy didn't know what was going through my head, so she said, "Sounds good to me. Ask Ms. Halliday and Miss Weber and Mr. Dougherty if it's okay with them."

So I did and it was. Their teachers even said I could be in charge. I think they were looking forward to the dance themselves. (Well, Ms. Halliday was. I had a feeling the other two just wanted to go to bed early. They'd looked tired ever since they'd come back from the hospital.)

As soon as I had the teachers' permission, I ran back to our dorm. "Guess what," I announced to the Conway Cove kids, "you guys are going to the dance, too!"

"We are?" they exclaimed.

"All right!" cried Ginnie.

"Will there be food?" asked Bryce.

"Definitely," I replied.

"We better get dressed!" said Pinky.

"Oh, you look fine the way you are."

"No, we want to look *good*," said Ian.

So the kids went about making themselves look *good*. From out of nowhere appeared hair ribbons and plastic necklaces. Joey had even brought a clip-on bowtie. (I got the feeling he had not done his own packing.) Then followed a flurry of hair brushing and shoe polishing.

"Are you guys ready?" Dawn asked when things had died down.

"Yup," replied Ian. "And," he added, eyeing his classmates critically, "we look *good*."

"Yeah. Good enough for a grown-up dance," said Pinky.

"Then let's go!" said Claud.

"Wait!" cried Mary Anne. "I want a picture of you kids."

"Okay!" they said eagerly.

Mary Anne posed the kids in two rows against a backdrop of bunk beds. *Click* went her camera.

Then Pinky said, "How about a picture of you guys? Our baby-sitters. We don't have a camera with us, but if I used your camera, Mary Anne, could you send us the picture later?"

Well, I could just about *see* Mary Anne melt. She nearly became a puddle on the floor of the dorm. And I didn't blame her. *Pinky* wanted a picture of *us*. She must have been getting over her homesickness.

Anyway, Mary Anne handed the camera to Pinky, Joey busily posed us BSC members, and *click* went the camera for a second time.

Then we were off to the dance.

My knees were actually shaking as we walked into the ballroom. Then I remembered that I had a job. The kids. I tried herding them over to the refreshment table, but the punch and cookies didn't hold their attention for long.

"Let's dance," said Ginnie to Kara and Amber. "Everyone else is."

That wasn't quite true. But with so many kids and teachers in the grand ballroom, it looked like the whole world was dancing. Before I knew what was happening, my charges were all out on the dance floor. Ryan danced with Ms. Halliday. Valerie danced with Rick Chow, the captain of the Red Team. Renée, Corey, Kathie, Frankie, and Ian danced in a group.

I looked around helplessly.

My mouth dropped open. Jessi was dancing with a seventh-grade boy!

Then — to my astonishment — Curtis swayed by. In his arms was a waitress from the dining room. Curtis was looking at her lovingly. At that moment I knew for sure that Curtis was no killer. He was just a regular old cook . . . and he was in love.

I stood by the punch bowl for what seemed like hours. Yes, this was the dance nightmare of the century. Everyone else looked so un-inhibited — the Conway Cove kids, the teach-ers, my friends, the people who worked at the lodge. Why couldn't I —

"Excuse me, do you want to dance?"

I was startled back to reality. A boy was standing in front of me. I recognized him. He was in my math class. Or maybe I'd just seen him in the cafeteria. Anyway, I was pretty sure he was in my grade. But he couldn't possibly be talking to me. I turned around. No one was behind me.

"I meant *you*," said the boy.

"Me?"

He nodded. "I'm Justin Price. We have math together."

I tried to smile. "Oh. . . . Right. I'm — "

"I know. You're Mallory Pike. Come on, let's dance."

I let Justin pull me into the crowd. I tried to remember everything Jessi had shown me, but pretty soon I realized that it didn't matter much. The room was so crowded that no one

215

Mallory

was paying attention to anyone else.

Justin and I spent the rest of the evening together. I stepped on his feet four times and he didn't mind at all.

Why had I ever worried about the dance?

CHAPTER 22

Stacey

Friday night

Mary Anne, I hope you don't mind if I don't tell you everything about the dance. Some parts are just too personal. I'll tell you as much as I can, though.

I guess it was no secret that Pierre and I wanted to spend the whole evening together. It was probably going to be the last time we'd see each other so we wanted the night to be special. Too bad we didn't know about the dance before we left for Hooksett Crossing. If we had, I would have brought along a special outfit. Oh, well. What really mattered was Pierre and me....

I'm not sure how it feels to be in love with a boy. Do you feel like you want to be with him every second? Like you and he are the only two people in the world? Like you've known each other all your lives, even though you just met? . . . Like your heart will break if you have to say good-bye to him?

If the answer to these questions is yes, then I was in love with Pierre, and had been since I first met him. It was a wonderful feeling, but scary, too. As soon as I "had" Pierre, I was afraid I'd lose him.

One of the nice things about Pierre was that I could talk to him the same way I could talk to my friends in the Baby-sitters Club. We could tell each other about our feelings — about times when we had been hurt or we were frightened, or about our feelings for each other. So I knew Pierre was wondering if he was in love with me, just like I was wondering if I was in love with him. We'd talked about it. But we didn't have any answers.

Who would have thought that falling in love could be so hard?

Anyway, Pierre and I knew that Friday night would probably be the last time we'd spend any meaningful moments together. We'd get to say good-bye on Saturday, of course, but that wouldn't really count. It would be a hectic mess, and besides, tons of people would be around. Then the buses would leave, and Pierre would go back to Vermont and I would go back to Connecticut. There would be hours between us. We knew there wasn't much chance that we'd see each other again. We wouldn't even be returning to the lodge the next winter.

I couldn't decide whether to look forward to the dance. On the one hand, it would be our last chance to be together. On the other hand, it would be our *last chance* to be *together*. Is that what is meant by "bittersweet"?

I made myself look as nice as possible for the dance, considering that my wardrobe consisted mostly of pants and ski sweaters. Luckily, I had some makeup and jewelry with me, though. I managed to end up looking passable, particularly after I borrowed some fancy hair clips from Claudia. Anyway, Pierre hadn't seen me in anything dressy all week, so what did one more night matter?

Well, I suppose I ought to cut to the dance now and get to the juicy parts. By the time my friends and I led the Conway Cove kids down to the grand ballroom, the dance had already started. Most of the other kids were there, and Pierre was hanging around the entrance, waiting for me.

"Hi," I said softly.

"Hi," he replied. And before I knew it, we were in each other's arms, dancing across the floor.

We really wanted to spend the entire evening that way, but we knew it would be rude to look too exclusive, so we tried to trade partners every now and then. We also tried hard not to think about the awful thing that was going to happen the next day.

When we'd been at the dance for about an hour I said, "Pierre? Can we take a break? I'm getting tired. And thirsty."

"Sure," he answered.

We made our way to the punch table, which wasn't easy since the room was so crowded. As we squeezed between couples and dodged arms and legs, I noticed a few interesting things. I pointed them out to Pierre after he had gotten some punch for us and we were standing near the table, just watching people and enjoying being together.

"Look," I said. "There's Mallory, and she's *dancing*. With a *boy!*"

Pierre had barely spent any time with my friends, but he knew all about them because we had talked so much.

"Her first dance with a boy?" Pierre asked me.

I nodded. "She was so nervous tonight that she almost didn't come."

I kept watching the crowd. "There's Pinky," I said.

"Which one?"

"The little kid dancing with Jessi. A few minutes ago she was dancing with Mr. George. She sure loosened up."

"I hope those kids had fun this week," said Pierre.

"You know, I think they did — once they got over the shock of the accident. I mean, they've been pretty active. They've been skiing and skating and traying. And I think they built every single snowman that's out on the lawn."

Pierre smiled. Then he frowned and leaned forward, peering into the crowd.

"What? What is it?" I asked.

"There's a kid on crutches dancing with one of your friends."

"Where?"

"There." Pierre pointed.

"Oh, my gosh. That's Kristy and Jay!" I explained to Pierre who Jay was. "Kristy felt awfully guilty this afternoon."

"Jay looks like a goofball," Pierre commented.

"Oh, he isn't," I answered, giggling. "He's nice. It took guts to go out there and dance on crutches, and even more guts to do it in order to show Kristy that he doesn't blame her for — uh-oh."

Now it was Pierre's turn. "What? What?"

"There's Guy and his whole family. Even the baby. Oh, I hope Claudia doesn't see them. She'll — Oops. Too late. She just saw them. And Guy saw her. Oh, he's handing the baby to his wife. Now he's walking over to Claudia."

"He's cutting in on that boy she's dancing with," added Pierre.

"Now Claud and Guy are dancing. Aw, that's nice. Claud looks like she's died and gone to heaven."

Pierre and I finished our punch and began dancing again. We could hardly believe it when the lights dimmed so that the room was almost dark, and Mr. George spoke into a microphone:

"This will be the last dance," he announced. "Mrs. George and I hope you've enjoyed the evening and your stay at Leicester Lodge."

Everyone cheered and clapped loudly, then grew silent as a dreamy slow number began. Pierre and I swayed back and forth, and I felt happy and safe with his arms around me.

"This is it," Pierre whispered to me, and his breath tickled my ear.

I knew what he meant. It was our last dance together. Time to say good-bye. But I wasn't sure I was ready for that.

"Do we *have* to say good-bye?" I asked, hoping I wasn't whining.

"No." His breath was tickling my ear again.

"Then let's not."

"Okay. Are we going to write to each other?"

"Maybe. Do you think there's any point?"

"Of course I do!"

I smiled and pulled myself even closer to Pierre. "Okay. Then let's exchange our addresses tonight. Tomorrow will be too hard. I'd hate to do it in a big crowd of people who are all exchanging their addresses, too."

"Yeah," Pierre agreed.

A few minutes later I wrote my address on the back of Pierre's hand, and he wrote his on mine. Then he kissed me gently and walked away.

I decided I would never wash my hand again.

EPILOGUE

Mary Anne

And so we returned safely to Stoneybrook. Boy, was saying good-bye hard. And we had so many good-byes to say. Everyone wanted to say good-bye to the Georges. The members of the BSC said good-bye to the Conway Cove kids and to Miss Weber and Mr. Dougherty, and they all said good-bye to us. Most of the little kids cried, and so did I, of course. Then Claudia had to find Guy to say good-bye to him and his family. The funny thing is, I didn't see Stacey and Pierre say good-bye...

225

As I mentioned in the book for Logan, we arrived home safely. The roads were clear by Saturday, and the weather was sunny and bright, so there were no incidents on the way home — unless you count the boys on our bus singing a very mean song one too many times and causing a teacher on board to yell at them so loudly his dentures fell out. The boys were singing a song that is supposed to go like this:

> "Alice, where are you going?"
> "Upstairs to take a bath."
> Alice, with legs like toothpicks
> and a neck like a giraffe.
> Alice got in the bathtub.
> Alice pulled out the plug.
> Oh, my goodness! Bless my soul!
> There goes Alice down the hole!
> "Alice, where are you going?"
> "To . . . the . . . floor!"

However, the boys were singing about Ethel Tines, this fat girl on the bus, and they'd changed the words to the song:

> "Ethel, where are you going?"
> "Upstairs to take a bath."
> Ethel, with legs like tree stumps

226

and a neck like a baboon.
(So it didn't rhyme.)
Ethel got in the bathtub.
Ethel pulled the plug.
Oh, my goodness! Bless my soul!
Ethel can't fit down the hole!

(They didn't have a finish to this version, and it was probably just as well. However, the song didn't prevent Ethel from eating three Snickers bars on the way home.)

Anyway, we finally reached Stoneybrook, and was I ever glad to see my father and Tigger again. We had a happy reunion, and Tigger purred practically nonstop all Saturday evening.

A couple of weeks after we'd been back, the members of the BSC started receiving mail. Here are some of the postcards:

Dear Jessi,
Hi. How are you? I read the book you told me about. The one called Pinky Pye. I liked it because the kitten had my name.
Love, Pinky
P.S. Thank Mary Anne for the photo she sent. My friends and I like it.

227

Mary Anne

DEAR STACEY,
    SEE? I TOLD YOU WE'D WRITE.
THANK YOU FOR YOUR LETTER. I'LL
NEVER FORGET OUR WEEK AT THE LODGE,
EITHER. IT WAS THE BEST ONE OF MY
LIFE. I LOVE YOU.
        -- BILL (JUST KIDDING. THIS IS
           ME, PIERRE, OF COURSE.)

(I'm not sure I would write "I love you" on a postcard where the mailman and your mother could see it.)

Dear Claud,
  Hi! How's it going? How was the lodge? Are you coming to Camp Mohawk again this summer? You never did let me know. I'm going back. Even if you don't go, promise me you'll wear those stupid teepee clothes for two weeks out of sympathy for me.
                Love, Will

My Dear Claudia,
    Hello from Leicester Lodge! Marie asked about you this morning. I

told her we would probably not see
such a marvelous skier as you for
a long time. However, Marie is
turning into quite a skier. She
went down a beginner trail by
herself the other day. Domitille
sends her love.

                                — Guy

Some important things happened after we
got home again:

1. Kristy got over losing the Winter War.

2. Kristy stopped feeling guilty about Jay.

3. Kristy and Claudia stopped being mad at
each other.

4. Jay got his cast off.

5. My dad and Dawn's mom went to a for-
mal dance together.

6. I finished my project on time, handed it
in, and got an A on it.

7. I collected the notes my friends had been
keeping at the lodge and finished my book for
Logan.

I guess the most important news of all was
that Logan and I were happily reunited the
day after us SMS students returned from Vermont. Actually, the reunion was probably
more sappy than happy. Dad and I drove to

the airport to pick up the Brunos, and as soon
as I saw Logan, I ran straight into his arms.
He had bought a coral necklace for me in
Aruba and had it ready so that while I was
hugging him, he fastened it around my neck.
Then we held hands all the way home.

Logan's little brother kept looking at us and
saying, "Ew, ew."

Twelve days later, I finished Logan's book.
It had taken longer to write than I'd expected.
I had to do a lot of editing. I realized I needed
to take out all the parts about my wondering
if Logan had found a new girlfriend, and about
the dumb letters I kept writing to him.

At last the book was finished, though. I il-
lustrated it as best I could (I'm not much of
an artist), bound it (with Claudia's help), and
presented it to Logan.

He loved it.

Oh, yes. One other thing. This is the ded-
ication in the front of the book:

For Kristy, Dawn, Claudia,
Stacey, Jessi, and Mal--
the greatest friends
in the world.

About the Author

ANN M. MARTIN did *a lot* of baby-sitting when she was growing up in Princeton, New Jersey. Now her favorite baby-sitting charge is her cat, Mouse, who lives with her in her Manhattan apartment.

Ann Martin's Apple Paperbacks are *Bummer Summer, Inside Out, Stage Fright, Me and Katie (the Pest)*, and all the other books in the Baby-sitters Club series.

She is a former editor of books for children, and was graduated from Smith College. She likes ice cream, the beach, and *I Love Lucy*; and she hates to cook.

THE BABY-SITTERS Club ®

by Ann M. Martin

☐ MG43388-1	#1	Kristy's Great Idea	$3.25
☐ MG43387-3	#10	Logan Likes Mary Anne!	$3.25
☐ MG43660-0	#11	Kristy and the Snobs	$3.25
☐ MG43721-6	#12	Claudia and the New Girl	$3.25
☐ MG43386-5	#13	Good-bye Stacey, Good-bye	$3.25
☐ MG43385-7	#14	Hello, Mallory	$3.25
☐ MG43717-8	#15	Little Miss Stoneybrook...and Dawn	$3.25
☐ MG44234-1	#16	Jessi's Secret Language	$3.25
☐ MG43659-7	#17	Mary Anne's Bad-Luck Mystery	$3.25
☐ MG43718-6	#18	Stacey's Mistake	$3.25
☐ MG43510-8	#19	Claudia and the Bad Joke	$3.25
☐ MG43722-4	#20	Kristy and the Walking Disaster	$3.25
☐ MG43507-8	#21	Mallory and the Trouble with Twins	$3.25
☐ MG43658-9	#22	Jessi Ramsey, Pet-sitter	$3.25
☐ MG43900-6	#23	Dawn on the Coast	$3.25
☐ MG43506-X	#24	Kristy and the Mother's Day Surprise	$3.25
☐ MG43347-4	#25	Mary Anne and the Search for Tigger	$3.25
☐ MG42503-X	#26	Claudia and the Sad Good-bye	$3.25
☐ MG42502-1	#27	Jessi and the Superbrat	$3.25
☐ MG42501-3	#28	Welcome Back, Stacey!	$3.25
☐ MG42500-5	#29	Mallory and the Mystery Diary	$3.25
☐ MG42498-X	#30	Mary Anne and the Great Romance	$3.25
☐ MG42497-1	#31	Dawn's Wicked Stepsister	$3.25
☐ MG42496-3	#32	Kristy and the Secret of Susan	$3.25
☐ MG42495-5	#33	Claudia and the Great Search	$3.25
☐ MG42494-7	#34	Mary Anne and Too Many Boys	$3.25
☐ MG42508-0	#35	Stacey and the Mystery of Stoneybrook	$3.25
☐ MG43565-5	#36	Jessi's Baby-sitter	$3.25
☐ MG43566-3	#37	Dawn and the Older Boy	$3.25
☐ MG43567-1	#38	Kristy's Mystery Admirer	$3.25

More titles... ▶

The Baby-sitters Club titles continued...

❑ MG43568-X #39 Poor Mallory! $3.25
❑ MG44082-9 #40 Claudia and the Middle School Mystery $3.25
❑ MG43570-1 #41 Mary Anne Versus Logan $3.25
❑ MG44083-7 #42 Jessi and the Dance School Phantom $3.25
❑ MG43572-8 #43 Stacey's Emergency $3.25
❑ MG43573-6 #44 Dawn and the Big Sleepover $3.25
❑ MG43574-4 #45 Kristy and the Baby Parade $3.25
❑ MG43569-8 #46 Mary Anne Misses Logan $3.25
❑ MG44971-0 #47 Mallory on Strike $3.25
❑ MG43571-X #48 Jessi's Wish $3.25
❑ MG44970-2 #49 Claudia and the Genius of Elm Street $3.25
❑ MG44969-9 #50 Dawn's Big Date $3.25
❑ MG44968-0 #51 Stacey's Ex-Best Friend $3.25
❑ MG44966-4 #52 Mary Anne + 2 Many Babies $3.25
❑ MG44967-2 #53 Kristy for President $3.25
❑ MG44965-6 #54 Mallory and the Dream Horse $3.25
❑ MG44964-8 #55 Jessi's Gold Medal $3.25
❑ MG45657-1 #56 Keep Out, Claudia! $3.25
❑ MG45658-X #57 Dawn Saves the Planet $3.25
❑ MG45659-8 #58 Stacey's Choice $3.25
❑ MG45660-1 #59 Mallory Hates Boys (and Gym) $3.25
❑ MG45662-8 #60 Mary Anne's Makeover $3.50
❑ MG45663-6 #61 Jessi and the Awful Secret $3.50
❑ MG45575-3 Logan's Story Special Edition Readers' Request $3.25

Available wherever you buy books...or use this order form.

Scholastic Inc., P.O. Box 7502, 2931 E. McCarty Street, Jefferson City, MO 65102

Please send me the books I have checked above. I am enclosing $_____
(please add $2.00 to cover shipping and handling). Send check or money order - no
cash or C.O.D.s please.

Name _____

Address _____

City_____ State/Zip_____

Tell us your birth date! _____

Pssst... Know what? You can find out **everything** there is to know about *The Baby-sitters Club*. Join the BABY-SITTERS FAN CLUB! Get the hot news on the series, the inside scoop on all the Baby-sitters, and lots of baby-sitting fun...just for $4.95!

With your **two-year** membership, you get:

☆ An official membership card!
☆ A colorful banner!
☆ The exclusive Baby-sitters Fan Club quarterly newsletter with baby-sitting tips, activities and more!

Just fill in the coupon below and mail with payment to:
THE BABY-SITTERS FAN CLUB,
Scholastic Inc., P.O. Box 7500, 2931 E. McCarty Street, Jefferson City, MO 65012.

The Baby-sitters Fan Club

❑ **YES!** Enroll me in The Baby-sitters Fan Club! I've enclosed my check or money order (no cash please) for $4.95 made payable to Scholastic Inc.

Name _____ Age _____

Street _____

City _____ State/Zip _____

Where did you buy this *Baby-sitters Club* book?

❑ Bookstore   ❑ Drugstore   ❑ Supermarket   ❑ Book Club
❑ Book Fair   ❑ Other_____(specify)

BSC791